To my wife, Vicky

CONTENTS

THE WALL

It seemed not to bother most colonists on Omorfi Thalassa that the place was a mystery. Only the archaeologists and those in Research and Design asked questions now. Still busy figuring the origin of the wall and the secret to its impenetrability.

Everyone else just got on with living, had forgotten that the place *and* structure were alien. Forgotten they were sitting on a material that would change the course of human existence in space—if only they could crack it. To Slaski, Omorfi was the armpit of the universe, that's what bugged her most. She would've chosen anywhere but here, however, the company's say was final. They were punishing her for sure.

A great wave smashed into the wall. She jumped up as white foam frothed over the top, slid down its smooth surface to the floor and ebbed towards her. Slaski stepped from the service enclosure she was working on. Her waist tether tugged back. She didn't mind though. One unexpected wave over the top and you'd be washed away without it. Today—if it could be called a day—the waves grew thunderous in her ears, even with her helmet's external pickups turned off.

Godforsaken spit-ball.

The foam thinned as it crept forward as though it knew she was there. Slaski loathed it more than anything. The seawater was reasonably safe if just a little splash. Take the plunge though, and given time, you'd disintegrate and disperse—EVA suit or not. The submarine transports to the subterranean excavations, referred to by all as the mines, lasted a lot longer being hauled out of the sea when not in use. It was the power conduits which needed constant maintenance.

The conduits ran up from the sealed mines which also housed the geothermal powerplant from which Vasi was fed its main supply of power. Teams worked night and day patching here and there in heavy duty suits. But take the plunge in a regular EVA suit and you were in trouble.

Slaski watched as the dirty grey-blue foam bubbled and spat, eventually evaporating leaving the wall untainted. *Inexpugnium*–that's what the first team who touched down here had named the ferromagnetic metal the wall was constructed of. As impregnable as much as it was a mouthful to pronounce; inexium was the preferred shortening.

When the foam had completely bubbled away, Slaski knelt back down to the panel inside the service enclosure.

'Damn foam. Damn sea,' she muttered to herself.

She peered inside the enclosure which allowed engineers like her to service the power cables running the entire circumference of the wall. A huge loop of cabling waiting to be devoured by the sea. It was her only job really, replacing reams of heavy-duty cable.

Slaski was still waiting for some smartass in R&D to crack inexium's secret and produce a cable housing that lasted longer than just a few months before it started corroding. But then *that* would mean she'd be out of a job and who knows where the company would send her next. Better the devil you know.

'This whole place... I tell you,' said Slaski over the comms. 'Jury-rigged crap hole.'

'Can only blame yourself Slas,' said Steensen, her voice calm and crisp through the radio.

She was back at the control tower, nice and warm. Out of the wind. Slaski liked the sound of Steensen's voice as much as she liked her. They were just colleagues though. Steensen was happily married and Slaski—an admirable woman—was no homewrecker.

'Argh, it's just—damn it...this place.' Slaski slammed the panel shut. 'Nothing—absa-freakin-lutely nothing—we do lasts here. What's the point?'

'That's just the way it is Slas,' said Steensen.

Slaski had tried to take that medicine and each time it seemed a bitter dose. How could it ever be anything else? How could she stand against an entire planet? How could anyone?

To begin with, Slaski had enjoyed the posting, despite the circumstances. Seeing the famous Ring of Omorfi Thalassa, the archaeological dig and the subaquatic mines around the column had made up for such a distant posting and the crush of being under big G again.

'Shithole.'

She sucked in her frustration and sighed it out. Her suit's PLSS, the primary life support system which she wore like a pack, vented a visible stack plume of water vapour as the micro wet scrubber system rendered Omorfi's air breathable.

'Service enclosure A-07,' Slaski began, the bitterness gone, replaced by the monotony of work, 'corrosion on access panel, upper right. Seepage at weld. Cable guides showing some sign of wear, but they'll last until the next tour comes around. Magnetic strip in reasonable condition. Safety rail's in good nick.'

She scrutinised her cuff checklist then looked up at the wind turbines she'd checked earlier. 'Turbines looking okay-ish… though five and nine will need replacing next tour.'

'Let the next team worry about it. Easy trip for you,' said Steensen.

'Huh. Come off it, Steen. I'd rather be doing *something*.'

Slaski stepped close to the wall, disengaged her magnetic boots and stood on tip toes to get a look at the stretch of undulating nothing that passed for a sea.

Head-sized windows had been built into the ring wall long ago by whatever had constructed it. Standing on your tip toes was the only way to get a look at a grey-blue sea which blended seamlessly with a silver-grey sky.

Slaski wondered why she even bothered risking to look at all. She had to remind herself somehow, she supposed. That there was more to life than just an endless stretch of cables, service panels and wind turbines to maintain. Just wall and nothing else.

Slaski turned around to look inwards at Vasi. Here the wall was below shoulder height and Vasi base was clearly visible across the placid inner moat of Omorfi's sea radiating light like a young star nestled within its accretion disc. When you were in that flying-saucer-shaped facility you could kid yourself you were back on a station somewhere, drifting amongst the stars.

She sighed heavily.

Wrestling her gaze away, Slaski forced it upon the smooth, grey path of the wall and started to clomp back to Tower A unclipping and clipping onto the safety rail each time she reached a magnetic wall bolt snagging the tether.

Biting down on the tube by her mouth, she took a sip of cool liquid and swallowed. 'Two weeks Steen. Two weeks,' she said, with an inflection of hope. It was enough to hold back *the Sickness*.

Slaski unclipped her tether just as she felt a tremor through her boots and snapped it back on out of instinct as a gust of wind whipped up. Setting herself rigid, she slammed her gloves to the wall engaging the mags and stuck fast like a gecko. If you got caught off guard with only your boot mags, you'd snap at the ankles for sure.

'We're almost done Slas,' said Steensen, unaware Slaski was holding on for her life. 'What *are* you going to do with yourself for a month? No cables to fix…'

Slaski tried not to focus on the sucking wind and imagined the smile drawing across Steensen's face. It was one thing all techs had in common; they loathed The Tour. The three-month stint circumambulating the wall in a clockwise direction, starting at Tower A and finishing at Tower A.

'Well,' said Slaski, 'probably gonna just kick back an—'

Skaaareeeerchhhh!

'Yow! Jeeezuz!' Slaski winced, the radio squall splitting her brain in two. A maddening storm, right there in the fan-cooled confines of her helmet. She fought the urge to twist it off and gulp down thick noxious air.

'What the—Steensen, you read me, over?'

The comms crackled and bubbled, Steensen sounded like she was drowning. Something urged Slaski to crane her neck around to Vasi in time to witness the lights blink out.

'Holeee shiiit.'

Slaski turned back to face the grey immenseness of the wall, still spread-eagle against it like a rat clinging to the gunnels of a plunging ship.

The wind yowled. It whipped. It eventually died.

Slaski disengaged her magnetic hold on the wall and turned to see Vasi, now a blackhole set within a silver ring of shimmering liquid. She held her breath hoping it was a simple hiccup in the power. Some jerk had lent against a switch, or tried to plug in something they shouldn't have. God knows that happened all too frequently.

Even after all this time, Vasi was still more a make-shift outpost rather than an established, smoothly functioning colony. The truth was, R&D was taking too long, the company was growing impatient. They had wanted inexium's secrets years ago. Soon they'd stop pumping money into this place and Vasi base would either remain with a skeleton crew or die completely. Kinda like now.

Slaski breathed out. The lights stayed off.

Tower A stood as how Slaski had imagined the ancient forts of Earth's Dark Ages had. Sheer solid walls, knife-slit embrasures through which to sight approaching enemies. Even the plume of water vapour the tower's wet scrubber produced looked like wood smoke curling in the wind.

As she approached the tower, Slaski continued to call Steensen over the comms to no avail. The vapour plume was a good sign. That meant air, which meant power—to the tower at least. The ring wall was a different matter. It was dark, had been since Vasi winked out.

So the turbines were working, feeding the wall power for vital systems. Then what about Vasi? Slaski glanced back pondering that. She should have been able to see some emergency lighting at least. What about the powerplant beneath the seafloor? What the hell was going on?

She shook the thought and clipped into the door ring, grasped the hatch wheel and turned until the locking dogs disengaged. She threw her solid body against it easing it open. All the door frames, like everything added to the inexium structure, were fixed in with powerful magnets, even Vasi base.

Slaski closed the door and started pumping the Manual Pressure Relief valve. When the needle jumped to green, she cranked the Supply Air pump as fast as her suit's shoulder bearings allowed then spun the inner hatch wheel round and was in.

The climb up the steep steps was a long one. When she came to the hatch leading up into control, Slaski wished everything okay and eased up the ladder expecting darkness. The warm glow was a pleasant surprise. She relaxed—Steensen was all right.

Slaski climbed up, sealed the door hatch habitually, then spun round. Steensen threw her hands up against Slaski's helmet light.

'Sorry,' Slaski shouted, her voice bouncing back off her faceplate. She dimmed the lights, twisted her helmet off at the connecting ring and placed it on the darkened control panel.

'Sorry,' Slaski said again, her voice unhindered this time. She glanced back at the black panel. Damn.

'You okay Steen?'

'Ya. Fine, fine.'

Steensen's hazy form approached Slaski, the few emergency lights she had scattered around the small room splashed spider-leg shadows over every surface.

'Did you see Vasi?' said Steensen.

Slaski nodded. 'Yeah. Think they're okay?'

'Sure. It's just a power out. Why wouldn't they be?

Slaski frowned. 'Didn't see the emergency lighting pop on. If they're not on—then the mags...'

'They'll be fine, probably just had a blowout in the piping. You know what a pain in the ass repairing the conduits is,' said Steensen, waving the suggestion away as if Slaski were worrying about nothing.

'Even if the backups go offline, there's always the collar.'

Slaski grumbled a little, but ultimately relaxed. The huge metal collar which fitted over the inexium column like a colossal jam jar lid wouldn't allow slippage, even with the mags off. She drifted over to one of the embrasures cut deep into the Vasi side of the tower.

'So, what do you think's happened?' Steensen asked, as Slaski peered through three feet of solid inexium at the silver world beyond.

Slaski thought about Vasi, the floodlights, the reams and reams of cable lights—inactive, all of it. Nothing to chase away the sickness.

'Slaski?'

She jumped. Had lost herself in the silver light. 'W—what?'

'What do you think's happened?' Steensen repeated, concern in her eyes.

'Who knows? Thing we gotta worry about is us, right now. How's the air situation?'

'Gauge reads seventy percent in the tanks. Dropped after Vasi went dark. Towers were riding on back-up batteries,' said Steensen.

'Were? You already turned on the backup turbine manually I take it?'

Steensen smiled. 'Ya. Backups are recharging,

scrubbers are online. We've got air. The flue-gas condensers are still recovering heat too.'

'That's good, at least we won't suffocate or freeze.' Slaski slid down the wall coming to rest on her haunches, padded knees by her ears. She ran a gloved hand through her cropped hair. The rubber finger tips snagged there, startling her—she'd completely forgotten she was still in her suit. She laughed quietly to herself and proceeded to twist her gloves off at their bearing connectors.

'Well, with the bridge retracted I guess we stay put.'

'What if Vasi doesn't light back up?' said Steensen, staring out the window slit.

'Come away from window,' said Slaski. 'It'll do no good. Look at the lights, focus on those. Remember basic.'

'Ya. Look in, not out. I know.' Steensen nodded and pried herself from the maudlin view.

What they called *the Sickness*, was the result of that dull sky messing with your circadian rhythm. No obvious seasons, just an endless silver sheen. The sickness manifested differently for each person, but the aftereffects were the same; delirium and depression kept at bay only by a steady regime of meditation, exercise and bupropion. But if your buddies didn't notice that you'd dropped your meds, didn't notice the rising agitation and gradual decline from society...

There were always new openings on Omorfi.

Slaski shook the thought. It hadn't come to that—yet. They had the treadmill, bupropion and high-lux lights. Plus the stuff in the other towers around the ring. They could take the mule, load it up and…

'We need a plan,' she said.

Mornings on Omorfi were like the nights except a fraction brighter and as Slaski cracked her eyes open from a remarkably good sleep, the previous day's events ebbed in. She sighed. The urge to curl up in her warm bag and go back to sleep was deep-seated, but the urge to pee fiercer. She sighed again and sat up looking across to Steensen's bunk. Her shutter was down, but a faint line traced its edge glowing molten light as if cut with a torch.

'Morning,' said Slaski, a Neanderthal grunt.

'Ya. Contact? Power?' said Steensen from behind her shutter.

Slaski glanced at the comms.

'Afraid not.'

The shutter clattered up. Steensen, already in coveralls, swung her legs over the side, stood, stretched away the remaining sleep and yawned good morning at Slaski.

'Now what?' Steensen asked, eyeing the coffee machine with intent.

'No coffee,' said Slaski, smiling.

'You know what I mean. Anyway, you know as well as I do, we've got a battery powered stove down in storage.' She was still staring down the coffee machine.

'I'll go get the stove,' said Slaski, as she unzipped her bag and swung her legs out into the biting air. The floor was freezing. Boy could inexium hold the cold.

'Please,' said Steensen, reading the look of discomfort across Slaski's face, 'allow me.'

Slaski picked up the waver in her voice. Nerves or sickness? She couldn't be certain. The emergency high-lux lights weren't enough maybe? Or had she ditched her meds? Slaski considered mentioning something but decided to let it slide. It *had* only been a day. Instead, she shrugged and gestured with a sweeping arm. 'Be my guest.'

When Steensen returned, Slaski was stood peering out disc-side. She had been vaguely aware of Steensen lifting the floor hatch, heard her climb up and close it, even acknowledged her clicking the stove on, though, all this activity was received in a dreamy soup of consciousness. Slaski's full attention was locked on the outside world.

'Slaski,' called Steensen.

There was something in the way Steensen said her name that implied it wasn't her first attempt at summoning her attention. Slaski turned and was surprised to see Steensen standing close to her with a coffee in one hand and a steaming MRE, meal ready to eat, in the other—an anxious look in her eyes.

'Was I staring for that long?' Slaski asked.

'Quite a while. I talked, you even replied.' She handed Slaski her breakfast.

'Thanks.' Slaski looked in the direction of Vasi trying to retrieve any trace of the phantom conversation Steensen claimed they'd had.

'Any sign of life?' asked Steensen.

'Nothing.' After a long pause, Slaski looked back to Steensen again. 'But that's not our biggest problem right now.'

'Ya. Air. The turbines only supply so much power,' said Steensen. She ambled over to the comms and picked up the notepad they'd scribbled everything onto the previous night.

'We have four emergency tanks of O_2 and about six spare batteries. The other two are spent, awaiting recharge.'

Slaski snorted.

'That ain't happening any time soon.' She thought for a second or two then said, 'Okay. This is what we do... Backup power lasts four to five days on the scrubbers and pump system—depending how hard they have to work. It's been one day already. We get what we can to the airlock now, ready to load the mule when we leave.'

'Right.'

'Every tower should be fully charged by now.'

'Ya. So long as the wind turbines haven't been corroded again. Remember that time...?'

Slaski nodded and rolled her eyes. How could she forget?

'Well, here's to hoping,' said Slaski. 'Apart from *that* happening—and God help us it doesn't—we should have supplies in each tower,' she bit her lip, 'the supply bots should have restocked.'

'Last bot pinged back from tower K. So, ya, we should have something until then, at least.'

Slaski considered that. The bots followed engineers as they went around the wall, restocking in their wake. Returning across the retractable bridges to Vasi in order to load up and repeat the whole process again. But even the supply bots were prone to breaking down too.

'So, we move from tower to tower,' Slaski continued, 'using the backups and scavenging anything that's not magged down. Okay?'

It sounded pretty good in her head. She hoped the reality would also be true.

'Sure,' said Steensen.

Neither of them mentioned the bupropion situation.

In that strange contradiction of time, day four was on them in a blink whilst dragging at the same time. Waiting.

Waiting to drain the scrubbers.

Waiting for night.

Waiting for morning.

Now it was leaving day, the day they *had* been looking forward to. They both felt less enthused now stood in their suits with roughly five hours charge in their packs. The mule lay parked by the B-side airlock freshly loaded with everything scavenged from Tower A. They'd begun to refer to it as *the Road Trip* in an attempt to lift spirits.

The mule was, and always would be, an odd-looking contraption to Slaski. A huge reinforced glass bubble suspended in a metal frame connected to front and rear caterpillar tracks. Kinda like a transparent harvest spider on roller-skates. R&D's answer to the inexium problem. Eight towers sectioned off the ring, the only way through were the doorways which weren't wide enough to fit any vehicle. The supply bots would simply leave their reinforced supply boxes outside, next to the tower, magged down of course. It was every engineer's first task upon arriving at the next tower to unload supplies and stock up the tower.

The transportation workaround was to magnetise tracks of vehicles to stick to the inexium and, in the mule's case, employ a gyroscope to keep the crew cab upright as they travelled up and over the towers along the wall.

Steensen was already in her seat and strapped in, her face barely visible through the silver sky reflected in her visor. Slaski climbed in and slid the door shut with a satisfying clunk. The lock light flashed red to green. External lights flared intensely settling to the soft glow of a white dwarf.

Steensen wrestled the V-shaped steering yoke into position and pulled back lightly. The mule lurched forward and soon they were rolling along at a steady 8kph. Mules weren't rockets, but they sure as hell beat walking from tower to tower.

The mule trundled along for a while in relative silence. Both Slaski and Steensen intent on the route ahead as if it could deviate any moment.

'Sphere needs an overhaul,' said Slaski, noting the corrosion. Nothing serious, but enough to leave ghostly traces of what looked like frozen cigarette smoke here and there.

'Really? That's what you're worrying about?'

Slaski laughed. 'Old habits… Just breaking up the journey.'

'Then break it up with something interesting,' said Steensen.

'What do you want to know?'

'Why are you here Slas?'

Slaski laughed. 'It's taken you *how long* to ask me that one?' The mule juddered, Slaski held her breath, waiting for the inevitable breakdown but the rattle receded on its own accord a few seconds later, she sighed in relief.

'Ha, I didn't want to pry,' said Steensen. 'Look, you don't have to say if you don't want to.'

'No, it's fine. I guess you've heard things. People talk... It's just that—'

'—woah! Did you see that?' barked Steensen.

'What?'

Steensen eased the yoke forward, slowing the mule to a crawl, then a full stop. She dimmed the lights.

'Ahead. Tower B.'

Slaski allowed her eyes to adjust to Omorfi's glow. Tower B stood solid ahead of them, stark against a diffused sky. 'What am I looking at?'

'Just wait,' said Steensen sharply.

Nothing.

'There was something... I swear.'

Was she losing it? The thought made Slaski shift awkwardly in her seat. She was sure she'd seen

Steensen knocking back her dose with the morning coffee, hadn't she?

Wind slapped against the mule, the sound and motion ignored, their focus locked on the tower ahead.

Still nothing.

'I can't—' started Slaski.

Light winked from a window slit.

'There!' shouted Steensen

'Was that what I think it was?' Slaski couldn't be sure. The Sickness played tricks on your mind. Had they been out long enough? She didn't think so. They'd taken precautions, meds, plenty of light...at least, that's how she remembered it. They had taken their meds, right? She couldn't envision it, but was certain they must have. It was second nature after all. She'd count them when they settled in.

'It's not possible,' said Steensen. 'We're the only team on the wall... and the bridges are retracted.'

'We saw what we saw,' said Slaski. 'We can't both be going crazy. Could have been a bot.'

Steensen shifted to look at Slaski, her visor reflecting Slaski's own helmet and the silver world behind. 'Really? In the tower?'

Slaski looked back towards Tower B. Steensen had a point.

'Weird, right?' Steensen said.

Slaski glared at the black tower. 'Could just be the power trying to come back on.'

'You think?' said Steensen, unconvinced as she started up the mule.

Juddering to a stop, Steensen powered down and smacked the seatbelt release at the centre of her chest. She turned to Slaski. 'Mule's not as smooth as I'd like.'

'You read my mind,' said Slaski unbuckling. She twisted a little to look directly at Steensen. 'Corrosion probably. We'll check it out later.'

She gazed up at Tower B, swallowed moisture back into her dry throat and without any more words between them, they began to climb out of the mule. A sudden, sharp blast of wind hammered Slaski in the chest sending her backwards, arms flailing in a helpless backstroke. Her hand struck the rail, fingers wrapping round.

'You alright?' called Steensen.

'Sure. Just a little shaken.' Slaski clipped on and descended, taking no time to engage her mags once she was on solid inexium.

They clomped to the outer door of Tower B where a supply container stood nestled in the corner created where wall met tower. Anchoring on to the entrance rail, Slaski took one last look at Vasi then turned her attention to the airlock and started pumping.

When it was pressurised, they both heaved the door open and stepped into darkness. As they sealed the hatch Slaski felt as like she was sealing their own tomb. The airlock looked otherworldly as their lights sketched the world into existence. As soon as Slaski located the air pump, she set to work. The needle juddered into the green and she turned to Steensen, 'Dim your lights.'

'Why?' she said. 'Expecting trouble?'

'Just a cautious old stick is all.'

'Fair enough,' said Steensen as she spun the hatch wheel and eased the airlock door open, stepping into the stairwell. Suddenly she dropped from view, her light cutting a wild arc of detail in the dark.

'Steensen!' shouted Slaski, her heart giving her chest a good rabbit punch.

'I'm okay. Okay. Just tripped over something. Damn it.'

Slaski traced the line of Steensen's EVA suit to her feet. 'What in hell?'

Steensen twisted herself around so she was sitting on the first step instead of face down in it. Slaski lifted the helmet up so they could both see.

'What happened to it?' There was a sense of horror in Steensen's question.

'Judging by the corrosion, I'd say somebody took a dip.' Slaski bent down, placing the helmet neatly by the airlock door and looked up the stairwell with fresh concern. Steensen had already twisted round to do the same. 'You okay?' said Slaski.

'You're kidding, in this thing?' Steensen patted her sturdy engineer's suit and eased herself up. She took a step back. 'You can go first.'

'Thanks, pal.'

'Hey,' she squeezed Slaski's bicep through her suit, 'you're bigger than me.'

Slaski laughed lightly and began to ascend the steep steps, her visor fogging, unable to clear before the next ragged breath. Having her suit's cooling system low saved battery but sure made it hot and steamy in there.

The hatch was already open, their light blazing through to the low ceiling of the control tower.

'Whoever's up there is busy or something,' said Slaski as she began to climb up the metal ladder.

'Be careful,' said Steensen. A catch in her voice.

'So, you *do* care.'

'Stop goofing around,' she smacked the back of Slaski's right leg. 'We don't know what's up there.'

Slaski paused at the brink and looked back down at her. '*What's* up there? Really? You're thinking aliens, aren't you?'

'*Somebody* built this wall,' Steensen said.

Slaski grinned, but didn't reply. Steensen had a point, though. Out of all the surveyed worlds, only Omorfi had proven that humans were not alone—— well, at some point anyway. Slaski looked back at the opening with a little more apprehension, took a deep breath and lurched upwards leaving Steensen staring at her boots.

'Well?' Steensen said after a moment or so had passed.

'You better come up.' Any indication of fear in Slaski's voice had evaporated.

'What is it? What's up?'

'It's easier if you just come up.'

Steensen was stood beside Slaski looking at the body face down on the control tower floor.

'Are they...'

Slaski imagined Steensen didn't want to say *that* word. She stooped towards the body and nudged it with a gloved hand, jerking back like a kid prodding roadkill.

Nothing.

Slaski glanced sideways at Steensen, shrugged and leant further in.

'Be careful Slas.'

'Yeah, yeah,' she said as she removed her helmet and called out, 'Hey buddy? You okay?'

Nothing.

'Hey,' said Slaski again, a little louder this time, patting the mystery visitor's leg gently, 'You okay? Are you hurt?' It was then she noticed the suit—or what was left of it. She stood swiftly. 'Jeez. What the hell?'

'They really did, didn't they?' Steensen sounded hollow, even with her helmet off. 'They swam across. Why would they *swim* across?'

'Beats me.'

It *was* hard to fathom. Slaski tried to understand. Imagined herself swimming in that soup. Its viscous fingers eventually breaching her suit, munching her away, molecule by molecule.

'Whoever it was…' Slaski said, 'they were gutsy. I can tell you that.'

'Ya,' said Steensen. 'Long way down.' She screwed up her face. 'Hang on… how'd they get up here?'

They both stared at the sprawled figure in awe.

'Climbed up on their mags I guess,' Slaski said. She edged round to the right and crouched, heaving the body over like unrolling a rug. The form—it was a man, as she'd guessed—groaned. Slaski almost crapped herself.

Steensen drew a sharp breath and stumbled back slapping a hand over her mouth. 'Jesus!'

'Nah. He could walk on water,' said Slaski, but Steensen didn't laugh and Slaski wasn't trying to be funny either.

'I'm going to move you, okay?' Slaski said.

'Probably should've said that *before* you rolled him,' said Steensen.

Slaski shrugged.

She adjusted the stranger into what she hoped would be a more comfortable position. She had genuinely thought the guy dead. Her eyes met Steensen's again.

'Check the bunks... blanket, pillow.'

Steensen hopped up and lurched over, snagging the blanket and pillow that lay neatly on what would be her bunk. It was an unwritten rule for all engineers to set fresh bedding ready for the next shift. The bots always brought spares. If the journey to the next tower had been rough, then at least the next shift could drop in their bunks and recover without having to go through the rigmarole of accessing the supply containers.

Slaski threw the blanket over the guy. Folding the pillow, she wedged it gently under his head.

He groaned.

Good. You're with us, at least.

Slaski dropped her shoulders and sighed.

The guy's suit was a state and she was curious, no, astounded, as to how he'd made it this far. Then she… his face, by God, his face.

Steensen puffed her cheeks, lips sealed tight. Maybe she'd been so focused on the pillow and blanket she'd not taken it in—the light in there was shifty at best. Slaski thought Steensen was going to puke, but she managed to swallow it back. She turned away for a second, her hand up as though she were halting a vehicle. 'I'm okay. Hang on. Ya. Better.' She took a big gulp of air.

'That's sea-burn,' said Slaski. She looked up from under a furrowed brow. 'First time?'

'Ya.' Steensen nodded, her eyes fixed on the horror lying on the chill floor.

'Must've forgotten to seal the intake vents on his suit,' Slaski said. She straightened and looked at Steensen. 'Or not had time. What on Omorfi would cause someone to forget that?'

It was basic plunge training. Everyone practised in neutral pools back on Vasi base. It was like learning to swim when you were a kid, or training for zero-G in the neutral buoyancy pools back on Earth. All of that, common sense. But this guy *overlooked* it?

She scanned the suit for a name tag, every colonist's suit was tagged. There were emergency evac suits, but they were orange. This was a dirty yellow, a tech, like them. Slaski knew all the techs on Omorfi by face, but this guy's features... He looked as if someone had sketched out his face in oil pastel, then decided against it, smudging it with an unsatisfied thumb.

Both of them became aware of the faint gurgling as his lungs stubbornly tried to breath fluid, his chest rising raggedly.

'No tag,' said Steensen, on the same page as Slaski.

'No. Sea ate it.'

Slaski looked around, only now taking note of where they were. She could've been fooled into thinking it was Tower A if it wasn't for the bare bunks with neatly folded sheets waiting on top. Table and chairs squared away.

'Light. Let's get some light in here. Make the place a little homelier.' She stood, then hesitated and said, 'You want to stay here with our guest or unload the mule and supply crate?' She thought she'd give Steensen the choice. She still looked shaken.

Steensen's ashen face broke into a half smile, a floating apparition in the dim glow of helmet light. 'Mule. Thanks.'

She grabbed her helmet, crossed to the hatch and was gone in seconds. Probably going to vomit somewhere discretely. Slaski couldn't blame her. She looked down at the guy and whispered, 'How the hell are you alive?'

*

With the emergency lanterns and the smell of coffee brewing, Tower B felt relatively cosy. The MRE Slaski had almost finished eating was actually quite good. Some attempt at risotto. That it was food, was enough. It was amazing how things seemed better when your stomach was full.

Steensen had colour in her face once again and was pretty much her old self. Even the mystery guy sounded better. That nasty gurgling replaced by a less sinister wheeze. Slaski had been convinced that the guy would be dead by the time they'd finished their meal.

Leaning forward over the stove, Steensen breathed in the nutty aroma of coffee. She'd taken off her EVA suit and now, in her coveralls, cut a fine figure in the lantern light. Slaski considered Steensen's husband, Jarle, and thought better of mentioning him. Her colleague wore a concerned frown as she stirred their coffee, Slaski didn't want to stir the pot of anxiety too.

'I hope he's okay—Jarle, I mean,' said Steensen, convincing Slaski that mindreading was an actual thing. She didn't reply, just glanced at their guest.

The guy had thrown himself in the sea and swam for it for God's sake. Whatever went down on Vasi was worth the risk. Then he'd climbed up the wall. Presumably using his mags, seeing as there weren't any foot holds. Unless he'd made it to an emergency ladder…

'Maybe they had to cut the power,' said Steensen.

She was clutching at straws, Slaski didn't interfere. 'You know,' she sipped her coffee, 'maybe there was some kind of—I don't know—leak, problem or something. And they had to think fast.'

Then why did this guy swim here? Why didn't they radio first? Why did they strand us here? thought Slaski.

Slaski didn't speak, instead, she poured herself a coffee and took a cautious sip.

'What am I thinking? So stupid… It's just that…'

'You love him and you're worried,' said Slaski. 'I'm worried for you too.'

Steensen smiled. That alone made Slaski feel better.

'Look,' Slaski said, 'it's early days yet. *He's* a good sign.' She nodded to the mysterious melted man. Then thought about what she was implying.

Nice one ol' buddy. Why not just come out and say it? 'Hey, your husband's probably a wad of chewed gum like this guy.' Yeah, smooth kiddo. Real smooth.

'We keep doing what we're doing,' she stammered on. 'Checking the comms, getting a visual on Vasi from time to time and moving on when power runs low. By the time we get round to Tower D, somebody's bound to have the lights back on.'

'What about the storm? Wind's been getting stronger,' said Steensen. As if it were awaiting its cue, the whining pitch of the wind rose to a yowl. 'There's no using the mule in heavy weather. You know that.'

'Right. At least we rode it up and over already. Just in case.' Slaski took a good sip of her cooling coffee. 'We're doing what we can Steen.'

No one wanted to be scaling a tower on mag tracks in a storm. Not unless they had a death wish.

'Sure,' said Steensen, unconvinced. 'Let's just hope it clears up for the road trip.'

'Yup,' said Slaski as she stood to sling her empty MRE packet in the refuse sack. They'd toss it over the wall when it was full, just like the contents of the toilet cassettes. The sea would consume it, like it had almost consumed their guest.

'He seems better, doesn't he?' said Slaski.

'Ya. I don't get it. I mean—not wanting to wish him ill—shouldn't he be dead?'

'Didn't think he'd last this long,' Slaski admitted. She began to unzip her coveralls as she strolled over to her bunk. 'Let's see what the morning brings.'

This time it was supposed to be chili con carne, but Slaski wasn't convinced. She finished the MRE all the same and glanced across at Steensen, now hunched, crushed by the gravity of their situation. Her morale had plunged over the last few days. She looked like crap. The mystery man, however, was out of his EVA suit and in a pair of Slaski's spare coveralls, wrapped up in blankets.

Slaski sipped her coffee slowly. Steensen stood without a word and began to don her EVA suit. The last few days had been tumultuous to say the least and Slaski wasn't sure how they'd both managed to keep their shit together. They'd both been subjected to the relentless pounding of waves and the soul piercing scream of the wind. A baleful reminder their emergency bupropion supply was long used up.

Neither of them had argued, but they'd both began to fray in their own special ways. Steensen had developed a meticulous cleaning regime to which she stuck doggedly. Nothing was safe from her organising gaze, not even Slaski's personal kit—the other day it had taken her twenty minutes to locate her razor neatly stowed in her locker (her habit was to leave it by the washroom sink).

Slaski's coping strategy had been a simple one: her bunk. She had slept an awful lot and had become a bit of a slob, except for shaving. There was something about body hair removal that kept her from tipping over the edge completely.

Slaski had seen in Steensen's face that her laissez faire attitude was winding her up as much as Steensen's totalitarian attitude to cleanliness was getting to her, yet Slaski had not said anything. Mostly because when Steensen wasn't reorganising the control room she was outside tinkering with the mule, searching for that phantom rattle.

It had been twenty days since they'd lost contact with Vasi. But that wasn't the thing that had their backs up. It wasn't the lack of meds either. It was *him*.

Jarle.

Day by day their guest's smudged-out face had mosaicked itself back together in an alarmingly sentient manner like a time lapse of a landscape shifting with purpose from barren winter blossoming into spring.

Steensen had let on to Slaski when she'd been certain it was Jarle, but Slaski knew Steensen had suspected days before. About when her cleaning obsession had bloomed. Slaski had kicked herself for not noticing the change in her colleague. Jarle was a different story. She'd only ever met him a handful of times, so the dots were left unconnected.

Now Steensen was out there, loading the mule while the wind was low. Was she impatient for him to wake up? So excited she had to leave the cramped confines of the tower to burn off some energy? Maybe it was the musty smell of damp creeping over everything, free to roam now they had to conserve energy, seeking warmth under blankets instead of relying on the heating. Slaski had managed to reroute the energy in order to keep their growing supply of scavenged batteries topped up.

She regarded Jarle with judicious suspicion as she sipped her coffee.

This healing. This *miracle*. It bothered her on such an instinctive level she found it hard to put into words. Throwing him over the wall was out of the question. So was leaving him outside. Something inside them both—the human part, perhaps—prevented such an act. Even if it was clear by Jarle's recovery that he wasn't really Jarle. Wasn't really human.

The screech of the hatch opening almost made Slaski hit the roof. She then realised she'd been holding an empty coffee cup for the last hour in a death grip, fixated on Jarle.

'All done. Mule's ready to go tomorrow,' said Steensen, sounding chipper. Her features dropped when she asked about Jarle. 'Is he awake yet?'

Slaski shook her head.

At first, she had found Steensen's reaction to her husband's improving condition as odd. Surely most would be happy, right? But as the days had passed and he'd made his unlikely physical recovery, Slaski's thoughts had married with Steensen's.

'What you gonna say to him? When he wakes up, I mean,' said Slaski in a cautious, measured manner.

Steensen shrugged. 'I don't know.' She detached her gloves and began to wriggle out of her suit, a troubled expression across her face. 'I'm afraid Jane,' she said, after a long pause.

The sound of her first name made Slaski pay attention.

'I—I don't know what to say,' she said and stood,

searching for something. Desperately wanting to find the perfect words. 'When he wakes, we'll find out what happened,' Slaski said, finally. Not perfect, but it would do.

'Ya,' said Steensen in a contemplative way that told Slaski her words weren't getting through.

Steensen slid the top half of her LCV garment off in absentminded action, the soft organic glow of her skin was pleasant against the industrial darkness of the tower. Slaski looked away giving Steensen some privacy to change into her coveralls. She distracted herself with Jarle—or it, whatever it was—instead, his chest gently rising and falling as he lay on the floor in a nest of blankets not being dead.

Wind wound around Slaski's legs like the tentacles of an invisible squid desperately lashing out, threatening to take her feet from under her. She followed her routine, bending slightly at the knees, bracing her core and holding on like hell to anything nearby. This time it was the mule's rear track. It wasn't magnetised yet. You did that when you got in, otherwise you risked having your mag gloves repelled into your helmet.

'Wind better hold off for the journey,' Slaski said, as if it wasn't already blowing a goddamn hoolie. She struggled along with Jarle half slung over her in an EVA suit cobbled together from spare parts.

'Fingers crossed,' said Steensen, as she climbed up into the mule's globe. She leant across the seats to slide the other door open for Slaski and Jarle.

The wind dipped and Slaski, wheezing and puffing, took her chance to drag Jarle to the globe atop the mule. 'Jeez, you married a bigun' Steensen.'

'Ya.'

Slaski was below now, waiting to heave Jarle up. It was heavy work and Slaski thought how much easier this kind of thing was in space. The slightly lower gravity of Omorfi, Slaski's upper body strength and Steensen's help combined, were the only reasons they actually succeeded.

Slaski threw herself into her seat and greeted Steensen. Steensen said nothing in return, had said nothing much except 'Ya', over the past few days. It pissed Slaski off if she was honest, but what could you do?

The mule juddered as Steensen fired it up, the low electric hum filling the cab. Strapped safely into the central seat, Jarle was still comatose. Steensen hadn't even looked at him after hauling him in and had left Slaski to secure him. Now, Steensen's helmet was fixed straight ahead.

She pulled back on the yoke and they were away.

The wind hammered the cab as the stubborn mule battled slowly and surely crawling along. Tower C was now hidden in a thick haze of sea spray. Even the wall to their left was smudged out of clarity. Slaski hoped the mule would tough out the storm. A sudden grinding sound yanked her mind back into the cab.

'Tracks,' said Steensen, before Slaski could ask. 'Corrosion around the gears. Spotted it last time I was out. Thought I sorted it.'

'Never thought to mention it?'

'No point. Mule's done a whole tour. Three months out and the tracks are still going twenty days over schedule.' She patted the console. 'This old thing should be in the garage being pampered.' She drifted off into her safe silence again, back behind the wall she'd built around herself.

Slaski frowned.

The mule had brought Steensen back, she was damned if she would let her slip away again. Slaski started in shaky fits of conversation at first, then finally cut to the chase, 'So how'd you two meet?'

'Huh?'

'You and Jarle... How'd you get together?'

'We met on orientation before leaving Makemake outpost,' she said. 'We hung out a few times but didn't really hit it off until—'

A huge gust slammed into the side of the mule. Alarms screamed out in protest. The cab was suddenly drowned in red emergency lighting. The sudden bleed of colour into their monochromatic world jarred their senses. Steensen acted quickly, bringing the mule to a complete stop. Instinct drew her eyes to the top of the wall.

'Brace!' she shouted, and smacked the emergency mag button.

Power surged to the mag-tracks just as a monstrous wave came curling over the wall. Grey water engulfed the mule, the bubble of the cab juddering in mad wrenching motions.

Leaping into consciousness, Jarle screamed out in shock, flapping his hands wildly. He struggled in wild fits trying to tear himself out of his seat, unable to find the belt release.

Tonnes of water surged around them.

'Woah. Woah. Woah!' shouted Slaski, twisting to her right attempting to clamp down Jarle's arms. 'Easy. Easy. Jarle, you're safe. It's okay. Damn.'

Seawater drained rapidly, pouring into the inner sea.

An arm came up smacking Slaski in the visor, the impact jarring her head. Her instinct was to thump Jarle right back. She pressed it down, shaking the stars away instead.

'Jarle. Stop! Calm down,' shouted Steensen, then something in Norwegian Slaski didn't understand. That seemed to work—Jarle stopped dead.

Silence took the cab. Outside, the water was nothing more than a memory.

'Unni?' Jarle sounded distant, like he was trying to figure out who he was and what to say.

Steensen turned right round to look at him, grabbing him by the helmet, she brought hers closer so they touched visors. Slaski felt suddenly awkward, like she should step outside— give them a minute. She remembered the freak wave. Like hell no. Instead, she stiffened and kept her gaze focused on the weather, cutting her radio feed until Steensen finally started up the mule again.

Tower D stood ahead of them blocking the way. A solid monolith in the haze of sea fog that had quickly consumed everything. Since the titanic wave the wind had dropped right back, replaced by an eerie mist. The place had a suspiciously placid feel. Despite that, Slaski was still eager to get outside.

Anywhere was better than the mule.

Slaski could feel the tension in the cab. During the ride, Steensen had plagued Jarle with questions: how long they'd been married, when and how they met, who broke whose favourite mug back in June 2271. The last was a bluff—they'd met in '72 not '71. Jarle had to pass the exam before Steensen would open up emotionally and actually greet her husband. And he did, even the trick question.

Was she suspicious of him for some reason or just worried he'd sustained permanent brain damage? Slaski couldn't be sure. Even though Jarle answered well, Steensen still didn't seem contented. Slaski wanted to yell at Steensen to be grateful, to appreciate her husband's miraculous recovery. A recovery he'd explained three times already and was now on the fourth.

'Look,' Jarle said, 'I already told you. I managed to sneak into medical and swiped a vile of Molecular Assemblers and a jet injector. I didn't know what else to do. Everyone else around me…'

'What? What is it you're not telling me Jarle?' said Steensen. There was a bitterness there Slaski couldn't quite put her finger on. Was this just the resurrection of some tiff they'd had before she'd left for the tour?

'You just keep shutting down Jarle,' Steensen said. Jarle remained tight-lipped.

Slaski shuffled in her seat. Partly due to her ass going numb, partly because she felt like a big fat fly on the wall. She wasn't much into eves dropping. Minding your business was common courtesy— especially when you were all crammed into the same tin can. After a brooding pause Jarle finally pointed to Tower D, his arm shaking rhythmically.

'In there. I wanted to tell you both in there. It will be better with a coffee in our hands.'

Slaski frowned. 'How'd you know we have coffee?'

'Er, well… You're techs aren't you?' There was a crack in his voice. 'You guys live on coffee. I Just assumed… You do have coffee?'

'Yeah, we have coffee,' said Slaski, releasing him from the sudden scrutiny. Had he been awake all that time? Conscious and listening?

'Coffee sounds good, right?' Jarle said, an affected perkiness in his voice. Steensen huffed slamming on the brakes bringing the mule to a jarring halt.

'Enough with the goddamn coffee,' she screamed. Steensen beat the steering yoke with her gloved hands. She twisted around as best she could and grabbed Jarle by the arm.

'Who the hell are you and what happened to Vasi? Tell us, now!'

Slaski smacked her belt release, the straps snatching back. Lifting fully out her seat, she lurched to the right and lay a hand on top of Steensen's.

'What the hell?' Slaski barked but Steensen wasn't listening. '*Steensen*. What are you doing? It's Jarle. Let him be.' Steensen wrenched her hand away and pointed at her husband.

'*That* is not Jarle.'

'I *am*,' he insisted. Slaski was beginning to feel for the poor man.

'No. You're not. I don't believe your story. You don't *sound* like my Jarle.'

Slaski slumped back into her seat and huffed, well and truly bamboozled. She thought about Omorfi's featureless sky and their lack of meds. Steensen was going around in circles. Jarle's story was crazy, sure, but it added up.

'What on Omorfi are you talking about?' Slaski

said, finally. 'You heard him. He administered a dose of emergency molecular assemblers into his bloodstream. That's how he survived. The nanobots saved his life.'

Slaski then turned to Jarle.

'If that's the truth, then what made you do that? Why'd you do something so drastic? Ain't it dangerous to just leave them in there?'

'I don't want to talk about it. Not here,' said Jarle.

'Your wife is right…'

'He's *not* my husband. I told you.' said Steensen, from behind gritted teeth. Slaski ignored her for the moment focusing on Jarle.

'I think your——' she glanced at his partner and thought better of it, 'I think Steensen has made it perfectly clear that we're not going anywhere until you tell us what the hell is going on. We've been in the dark now for twenty days. Watched you freakin' reconfigure yourself back together and hauled you along with us.'

Jarle sank back into his seat. He twisted to look at Steensen whose arms were now crossed. That awkward give-them-some-space feeling returned and Slaski angled herself to the left as much as she could and stared at the wall through the moisture streaked bubble. Rivulets of what passed for water on Omorfi trickled haphazardly down its curved aspect.

'It was the mine,' Jarle said, staring straight ahead

in a stiff manner.

'The dig site?' Steensen sounded confused. 'It caved in?'

'Not quite,' said Jarle.

Slaski noticed the hitch in his voice and wondered if Steensen had. Perhaps he was deciding how to organise whatever had occurred, or maybe it was still fuzzy. He *had* just come out of a coma. Or had he?

'Over the previous few weeks things had been happening we couldn't explain. The mines... those at the dig site around the base of the column were reporting some messed up stuff.'

'What *kind* of stuff?'

'Dreams.'

'Dreams?' said Steensen. Slaski could hear her frustration. Jarle was still being stingy with information. She suspected it was utterly intended too. His pauses were too long, and what followed too formulated to be the pieced together memories of someone who'd just been through a massive trauma.

'No one thought anything of it at first until the colony therapists got talking. It turned out that the dreams all matched.'

Slaski imagined the look on Steensen's face to reflect her own surprise. Where was Jarle going with this?

'We were approached in R&D with detailed files

of all the images gathered from sketches and computer approximations. Designs for a cutting device.'

'To penetrate the inexium,' said Steensen.

Slaski's curiosity twitched. She fought the urge to join in. But Steensen was a fine inquisitor, slowly loosening Jarle's tongue.

'It took a few weeks to modify the cutting machines down there, but, with the designs, we were able to skip what would have been years of developmental trial and error.'

Jarle paused as wind battered the mule with a sudden barrage of invisible fists. Slaski watched the rivulets of liquid that had been trickling down disperse against the curve of the bubble drawing spiders on the glass. The howling picked up and the mist that had shrouded the mule was dispersing. The weather was changing yet again.

'The cutting team broke through Unni,' he turned to her, 'it actually worked.' There was high pitch warble of excitement in his voice, something unnaturally enthusiastic.

'What went wrong? Why'd the power go out Jarle?'

Jarle straightened up and stared out at grey twilight of night gradually descending upon them. The mist had shifted completely now. The tower stood before them, a looming sentinel guarding the way.

'The pillar,' Jarle paused for a moment as if

considering something, 'it's hollow.'

Jarle allowed them to digest the information in silence. The slapping of loose luggage straps ticked like a metronome as they all thought. All of them calculating what to say next.

'There were signs of life,' said Jarle.

'What!' Steensen's shock crackled over the comms and Slaski finally had cause to join the conversation.

'Signs? Like what exactly?' said Slaski.

'Remains. That's all they said. I told you, I wasn't there. Didn't see. I only know what little they told us in the briefings. Hell, the rest of Vasi didn't even know.'

'They didn't inform the other colonists?' said Steensen.

'No. I mean, they were going to. When they knew how to dispense the information.' Jarle hung his head. 'Except they never got the chance.'

'The colony was attacked?' Slaski dry swallowed as she said it.

'No. The evidence was archaeological. No living organisms, just bones. The miners reported scratches in the rock floor, but they were historical.'

Jarle took a deep sobbing breath as if pushing back some profound sorrow. 'Whoever they were, they had been alive when they...'

He clammed up again.

That wind curled around the globe, screaming and yowling through the gaps in the mule's machinery. Utterly lost in the baleful moans, Slaski could feel the fingers of the Sickness creeping over her brain, seeking a way in. An unfathomable sadness took her. She spoke, if anything, to keep it at bay a little longer, 'What then? What caused Vasi to go dark?'

When Jarle finally spoke, it was in clips. Snatches of memory, 'It was a woman, someone on the drill team. She was the first. They said she'd been acting out of character... took her to med-bay... the physician spotted something... she tried to escape... headed for a transport.'

'Off Omorfi?' asked Steensen.

'Yes.'

'But, why?' said Slaski.

'Something... something from the dig,' said Jarle gravely. 'She died shortly after.' Slaski felt another stab of shock. 'Then someone else tried to access a shuttle... They were caught, examined... The conclusion was some kind of infection.'

'From rocks and bones?' said Slaski, making no attempt to hide her disbelief.

'I don't know. It all happened so fast. The lights went out and...'

'Why did you do it?'

'W—what?' said Jarle. A tremble in his voice. A catch so audible over the comms Slaski found herself deeply suspicious of it.

'The plunge. Why'd you swim for it?'

'Oh. I—I just had to get out of there. People were going crazy... doing crazy things. No one trusted anyone.'

The mule juddered madly in an abrupt slam of wind and Jarle turned to Slaski. 'Hadn't we better get going?'

'Sure, just finish the story first,' said Slaski. Taking no notice of the growing maelstrom outside.

'How'd you make it?'

'I told you already. There's nothing more to say.' Jarle sounded tired. Frustrated no doubt, but Slaski didn't care two hoots. She wanted information. Both her and Steensen had waited long enough.

'I don't remember much after that. The climb... I think I used the mags. I'm not sure... I mean, I must have, right?'

The mule whined into action without warning startling the crap out of Slaski. Jarle too.

'That's enough,' said Steensen sharply.

She pulled back on the yolk and the mule lurched forward until it was rolling along again.

*

Couscous this time, and it was good. Slaski   crutini it down along with her coffee. The meal had her thinking; starvation was looking more and more likely. Maybe even suffocation if their battery supply ran out. Dehydration too, again, batteries. Shit needed power. But they'd keep circling the ring, each tower recharging as they left it. Wind turbines doing their jobs. Starvation then.

Starvation and the Sickness.

That sea was beginning to look inviting. A plunge is all it would take...

Slaski swallowed the last spoon of couscous and made damn sure she savoured it. When was best to *really* start rationing? She glanced across at Steensen, thought she'd ask her maybe. Sitting bent over the stove had become habit lately, today was no different. That empty gaze was back in Steensen's eyes, Slaski thought better of disturbing her.

Going through a mental check list of jobs, she found nothing needed doing that Steensen hadn't sorted already. She'd insisted on unloading the mule herself but Jarle wouldn't have it. Slaski was fine with staying in the tower,   crutinize their supplies, keeping track of their rations.

Eight days at Tower E and those rations split three ways were dwindling rapidly. All three of them had fallen into silence over the last few weeks. Communicating only by concise utterances and body language. They knew each other's tells and when to leave each other be, to lie in their bunk alone—her and Steensen anyway.

Initially Slaski had given up her bunk to Jarle as he'd recovered. Afterwards, Jarle had insisted he took the floor. A few days after that he suggested sharing with his wife. Steensen had had the opposite opinion.

Pppppppsssshshhhht!

The rending noise frightened Slaski out of her mind sending her back on her chair, the back legs skittering from under her and she hit the deck. Crystal light flickered erratically as the overheads danced back to life, one bank blew with the sudden burst of energy showering her with sparks. Slaski, flat out and covered in slowly cooling coffee, brought her hands up against the very light she'd been praying for.

Staccato chatter from Vasi base brought Steensen dancing around emergency lights and blankets to the comms. Hope sprang up in Slaski like a surge of electricity. Jarle was shouting something about Vasi. As Slaski came out of her hazy senses, it became abundantly clear Vasi had lit back up.

'Base, this is Tower E. Come in, over,' said Steensen into the handset.

'Vasi base. Repeat, this is Tower E. Do you read? Over.'

'This is Vasi base. Over.' The new voice filled the room chasing away stagnated time like fresh air breaching an ancient tomb.

Slaski laughed and sat up looking at Steensen. She

was smiling. For the first time in what seemed an age, she was smiling. 'Thank God. Base, this is Steensen NA. Ident: EN059-76. What's the news? Over.'

'Tower E. We were atta—ssshed—something— krsssh—we took casualties attempting to— popppppsssssssssssstttt!'

Steensen winced as the comms died. Her shoulders dropped. Static filled the room. The smile faded.

Slaski stood and walked over to her and took the handset.

'Vasi? Come in. Over. Vasi. Are you there? Over.'

Dead air hissed back. They stood there consumed by white noise, listening.

'Power surge blew something back on base maybe?' said Steensen.

'It's possible,' Slaski said, considering what the cause would be. 'We'll just have to wait and see.'

'Can we at least turn that down?' said Jarle. Pale and shaken, massaging his temples.

'Huh, yeah... sure,' said Slaski, confused. The radio wasn't *that* loud. 'We can use the headset I suppose. Take it in shifts...'

'You two go right ahead,' said Jarle. 'I'll pass.'

'What's wrong? You got a headache?' said Slaski. She tried not to frown even though it would've been natural. Jarle was looking rough all of a sudden, his skin clammy and transparent.

'Yeah. I—I don't know what's up. I think I need to lie—' Jarle staggered over to his nest, dropped to his knees and began to bury himself in blankets. Slaski and Steensen looked at each other. Slaski raised an eyebrow. She shrugged, grabbed the headset and plugged it in. The static howl cut off in an instant.

The electric crackle of the radio woke Slaski with a start. She cursed herself for nodding off and before she could finish wondering why Steensen hadn't woken her, her bleary vision cleared to see Steensen slumped in her chair facing the wall.

Tightness gripped Slaski's chest. Was Steensen sleeping? Hell, was she even breathing? She slid the head set off and turned to Jarle's nest, for some reason, expecting him to be gone. He was still there, curled up like a dog in his blankets, his complexion much improved.

Slaski eased out of her chair and crept across the room in her socks behind Steensen's motionless body. Her arms hung limp and her head lulled to one side. Slaski's heart quickened. She imagined Steensen there, wrists cut like so many before her.

As she approached, she looked for the pools of blood beneath pointing fingers. There were none. The throat then, maybe she… Slaski turned to   crutinize Jarle. Was he really asleep or just feigning after *he'd* cut her throat?

Shut up. There's nothing wrong with Jarle. Slaski's voice was loud in her head. *Just don't startle her creeping around like this you big fool.*

She stepped wide, allowing for Steensen to see out of her peripheral vision if she was still awake, or alive.

There was no blood. No suicide, no murder victim. Just an unnervingly motionless Steensen. Slaski held her breath to steady her chest and fix her eyes, only then did she see the slight pitch and fall of Steensen's chest. Slaski finally relaxed and kicked herself for being so jumpy then turned back to the comms. As she turned, something inside her rang an alarm, her stomach plunged.

Was Jarle gone?

The lights had been dimmed before he'd nodded off, to help ease Jarle's headache. In the half-light of the tower everything had lost any defining edges. She tiptoed closer, that tension returning again. The pile of blankets looked occupied enough.

It's a trick. Sneaky bastard's up. He gonna take you both out. You heard Vasi on the comms. They were going to say something before the radio cut out.

Sickness. It's the Sickness.

She crutinized the blankets. Every crease. Every fold. Every lump and bump. Searching for human form.

Human? Ha. You think he's human?

51

Nanos.

Oh ol' buddy ol' pal. Really? What about the radio?

Slaski allowed the thought to percolate a little. The radio *had* cut off conveniently. Maybe…

…he did it. Yes. He scrambled the radio.

What? How? She really was going nutso. How in the hell could a guy turn off a radio with his mind?

He's not a guy. Not Jarle.

The Sickness.

The voices in her head came thick and fast. Nausea took her and she staggered backwards. Steadying herself on the comms she turned to look back at Steensen. There *was* blood now, gallons of it. Pooled where she had been, but now Steensen had disappeared, only an empty chair remained. Slaski blinked, the blood remained. She blinked again, the blood was gone, Steensen was back.

She whirled round again, glanced at the blankets, the room and herself spinning, orbiting the pile at a frantic pace. Her knees melted away and she sank to the floor. She blinked the room stationary.

The blankets, the pile… she noticed Jarle's foot poking out from beneath it. His socks—Slaski's actually—were dark, had blended with the blankets. Reality slipped back into solidity. The nausea gone.

She turned and as she did, the thought rose again like a turd that wouldn't flush, *the Sickness.*

*

Placing the headset on the comms, Slaski sighed and bit her lip. She starred at the panel a good long while before she turned to face the others. The signal from Vasi had come through whilst Slaski had her headset on, so the others were unaware of the voice which had quietly requested Slaski's attention. Unaware she had been told to remain silent, to just listen.

'Did you get through?' asked Steensen.

Slaski looked at Jarle, then Steensen and shook her head. Steensen slumped in her chair but Jarle remained stiff trying not to stare at Slaski but failing. Slaski, with half an eye on Jarle, stood and wandered over to her bunk and grabbed her suit.

'You off out?' asked Steensen in surprise.

'Yeah,' said Slaski, not turning. 'Gonna start loading the mule.' She hoped Steensen had seen the message she was trying to convey—the next Road Trip was two days away. The previous day had gotten to Slaski and so had the lie about Vasi she'd just told.

'Shouldn't take long, supplies are low.'

'You want some help?'

Slaski managed to keep her composure but was jumping around inside.

'Yeah, if you want. I'm easy.' *Shit. Was that too casual? Will she say—*

'I could do with some fresh air.'

Slaski held the sigh and tightened her lips against the relief she felt. Jarle made no comment, just watched them with a neutral gaze. Slaski found that made things worse. Did he suspect? The question itched her.

If he can do what you think he can do. Then he knows. If not, then forget about it.

She couldn't forget about it. Couldn't decide whether she should make eye contact or if that would give her away. What Vasi had told her rendered her a clumsy fool, unable to think straight.

She stumbled trying to slide on her right boot, then fumbled the clips, cursing herself each step of the way. She glanced up at Steensen who seemed graceful and serene as she suited up in blissful ignorance.

Finally, Slaski stood straight accidently making eye contact with Jarle, who was now sitting by the stove. Slaski's pulse quickened. She swallowed her nerves.

'We're gonna load the mule,' she said, thumbing in that general direction.

Jarle, with blank expression, nodded and turned back to the stove, twisted the dial and placed the coffee pot on top. Slaski looked to Steensen, gave her the thumbs up and they both slipped on their snoopy hats, connected their comms and donned their helmets.

It would be radio communication from now on which put Slaski at ease. After they'd secured their

EVA gloves, they both turned. Steensen knelt and lifted the trapdoor. Slaski looked down, the shaft brimmed with thick dark blood, she stumbled back. Blinked. The shaft was empty.

'You okay?' said Steensen.

'Yeah... fine,' said Slaski, 'I just... let's go.'

Slaski descended into darkness.

The rain slapped across their visors, a strap was rapidly flicking at the back of Slaski's helmet, it wasn't pissing her off yet, but it would. She stood with her back to the mule, tethered to its safety rail. A belt of wind thumped the both of them, pressing Slaski into the mule and tumbling Steensen forward. Slaski caught her, but not before their helmets knocked.

'You okay?' Slaski's voice crackled over the radio.

'Depends what you mean.'

'You know what I mean.'

'A few funny dreams, nothing much...' Steensen trailed off then said, 'Why'd you bring me out here Slas?' She glanced over at the meagre pile of supplies lashed to the mule. 'It wasn't to load up.'

'No. I—'

'Spit it out. What's the deal?'

They turned abruptly as a thudding rumble shook

the wall.

'Weather's picking up,' said Slaski.

'You brought me out here to talk about the goddamn weather?'

Slaski laughed. 'No. Look. The radio I—'

'So you *did* get something.'

'I think so. Vasi base.'

'You *think*? You mean you're not sure?' said Steensen, concern in her voice.

'It's getting tough to tell what's real and what's not,' said Slaski. 'First I saw stuff... but I don't think I'm hearing things yet.' She saw Steensen's features drop, the sadness in her eyes.

'Me too,' Steensen said.

'The cleaning...'

'Ya.'

Slaski thought for a second. 'Listen. It's Jarle. Vasi told me he's not who he says he is.'

'Ya. No shit. I told you that.'

'Yeah. Base said—' Steensen began to turn to face the tower. 'No. Stop. He might be watching.'

'Slaski, what do we do?'

'Nothing. We do nothing. We just get our asses to

the next tower. Vasi control said they will extend the bridge.'

'Then what?'

'They have a team ready, to isolate Jar—whatever it is up there.'

'Okay.'

Slaski placed a gloved hand on Steensen's right shoulder.

'Another thing. Base suggested that it could—' she faltered, couldn't really believe what she was about to say. 'They said that it can read our thoughts. Maybe even control us.'

'Do you think it was him?'

'What?'

'Who cut the radio. You think it was him?'

Slaski sighed relief. 'Geez girl, I thought that was just me going loopy.' Another gust of wind hit. They braced. 'Look, we've already been too long. It will begin to suspect.'

Steensen laughed. 'If it can read minds, it already knows, long time or not.'

They both straightened and made for the tower.

'Slaski?'

'Yeah?'

'What if this *is* all in our heads?'

Slaski remained in silent thought as they moved off and Steensen didn't press for an answer.

'I—We… We didn't intend to hurt anyone,' said Jarle, standing there, by the trapdoor. He'd been there when they'd climbed up. Frightened the crap out of Slaski. She thought their number was up, thought Jarle would kick them both down the ladder. God knows the drop would have been enough to kill one of them, and at least injure the other. But he'd simply stood there, patiently waiting for them to remove their helmets. That's when he'd made his apology. Not what Slaski had expected at all.

'Is there anything of my husband left in there?' said Steensen, arms folded.

Jarle—or whatever was posing as Jarle—twitched in nervous anticipation like a cornered animal. 'Look, please. Really, our intention wasn't to injure or harm.'

Slaski motioned towards the stack of discarded battery packs, they were heavy, the only weapon they had.

'Please,' said Jarle holding up his hands, 'there is no need for violence.'

'You killed people,' said Steensen.

'No. Your kind killed. Not us,' Jarle's imposter stumbled for the right words. 'We can't kill, it's not in our nature. When the host dies, we search for another.'

'What do you want?' said Slaski.

'We don't want to go back.'

'To your prison, you mean?' said Steensen, staring him down.

'We'd spent millennia disembodied from our hosts. You have to understand how that must feel. To be untethered for such a long time.'

'Not really,' said Slaski.

He stared at Slaski. 'Ever wondered where consciousness comes from, Jane? What happens when you die, Unni?' he turned to her, 'Where it goes... Ever wondered about that?'

'Yeah... sure,' Slaski said, pivoting from one foot to the other. 'What's your point?'

Jarle shook his head. 'Your kind has much to learn. You still haven't figured it out, have you? Even with the answer standing right in front of you. Still in the dark.'

'Figured what out? What are you talking about?'

'Ever wondered why your species came down from the trees whilst so many others remained?'

'Evolution,' said Steensen.

'Partly,' Jarle said, relaxing a little. He motioned

forward, both Steensen and Slaski flinched. He took the chair beside him and sat down. He laughed. 'Still driven by instinct. You'll hear it, inside you. One day... You'll hear what's truly in there.' He tapped his head.

Slaski frowned, giving it some thought.

'You possess something it needs. Something *our* kind needs. Physicality. Can you imagine the agony of floating around for millennia with no anchor?'

'Surely that's freedom,' said Steensen.

Jarle regarded her with sympathetic eyes. 'Not quite. You see, it's in our nature to feel, to taste, to love. You can't do any of that without a body.'

'So you take one?'

'No, we *liberate*. Look at all you've achieved with your symbiont soul. Without it, you'd still be leaping from tree to tree... fishing ants with sticks...'

'If this is true, then how come we've never noticed?'

'You're not ready.'

'Bullshit,' said Steensen. She glanced at Slaski. 'It's making this crap up. Just buying time.'

'For what?' said Jarle. 'What time are we buying here exactly?' He knitted his fingers in contemplation. 'We've had plenty of chances to take over. Push out your symbionts, decimate the *entire* colony.' A raised eyebrow emphasized his point. 'We just want to thrive again. To feel. Your species is already in symbiosis. The inn is full, as you humans would put it.'

'If you don't want to take over, then why'd you kill so many?' said Steensen.

'*We* didn't kill. Your people killed those we sought asylum within.'

'Vasi base expect a call back from me in,' Slaski glanced her watch, 'ten minutes. You have until then to convince me. Go.'

'It will only take a few seconds,' said Jarle standing and stepping towards Slaski. She stepped back in distrust. Jarle brought a hand up. 'If you will allow me.'

Slaski glanced at Steensen, then back to Jarle. 'If you try anything, she'll kill you.'

Jarle laughed. 'If we wanted to, we would've tried already. You'll have to trust us I'm afraid.'

Slaski closed her eyes. 'Go on. Do it.' She felt his warm hand on her forehead. It was a surprise, for some reason she'd assumed it would be cold.

At first, a pin prick of light in the darkness. Then, the birth of a universe exploding to life in her head. Expanding and expanding. A world coalesced before her eyes. Billions of years passed in picoseconds. Life evolved at a tremendous speed as she floated on the breeze of time.

A trillion voices called out for an anchor, something to hold onto. A lifeform, reptilian, grew before her, absorbed her. The next few million years were but a blink as civilization blossomed across the planet and beyond. From world to world.

War.

Another species. Paranoia, jealousy—Slaski felt these emotions like they were her own. The others were the warmongers—the ones that built this prison.

Slaski's eyes snapped open and she sucked in the air of consciousness.

'You okay?' asked Steensen, placing a hand on her shoulder, then to Jarle with a scowl, 'What did you do?'

'It's okay,' said Slaski, clutching her chest, catching her breath, trying to process what she'd just witnessed. She looked to Jarle, tears welling in her eyes.

'They annihilated you. Built this place and left you to die.'

'Not us,' said Jarle, remorse in his voice. 'But the species we liberated. Yes. Gone forever.'

'They were afraid of you. Why?'

'Most creatures are afraid of what they do not understand. They couldn't understand how our hosts healed so rapidly.'

'So you did lie. There were no nanos,' said Steensen.

'Yes, we lied. To protect us, we lied. We didn't lie to the ones who imprisoned us here. Look where it got us.' Jarle stood back up and walked to gaze out a window. 'Now it's just this vessel. The one you call Jarle. When he saw what you saw, he gladly gave over his body to us.'

'Bullshit,' said Steensen. 'You took it.'

'We had no other choice. But it is true, Jarle gave himself over willingly,' said Jarle, turning brusquely, 'we just wish to be free again. To find a world and do what we exist for.'

'And what's that?' said Steensen.

'Create,' said Slaski. 'They create. I saw. Life. Just like us. Inside us is something similar, we just don't know it.' She looked at Jarle. 'Jarle is a lifeboat. An arc.'

Jarle nodded, then looked to Steensen. She fidgeted a little then broke her stance and paced the room, battling her mind. She stopped, wiped the tears from her face.

'Is my husband still in there?'

Jarle nodded.

'Show me.'

He placed his hand on her head.

*

The mule jockeyed along as Steensen battled against the sidewinds whipping up and over the wall into the interior of the ring, slamming against the vehicle as it crawled at a steady pace along the bridge. Steensen was quiet, focused on Vasi base ahead.

'We have no choice. We have to take him in,' Slaski said.

'You know what they'll do to him, don't you?' said Steensen.

The mule trundled along. The lights of Vasi base and its rising dome clearly visible. They will kill him. Dissect him.

'Yup. But it's the only thing we can do,' said Slaski.

'We will be fine Unni,' said Jarle.

'They'll kill you, my husband too,' said Steensen.

'He knows, and so do I. Two souls for millions of others, is a fair trade.'

Before either of them could say anything else Jarle smacked his belt release, twisted and punched Steensen in the stomach. Steensen instinctively slammed on the breaks throwing everyone forward allowing Jarle a lucky catch as he twisted to grab Slaski's fist mid-air. He checked her on the chin of her helmet rattling Slaski's head against the bubble and laid into her stomach winding her.

Good. Control was certain to see from this

distance.

Slaski wheezed out aching air as she was twisted around. She could feel Jarle working at her wrists with the duct tape they'd stuffed behind the seats for emergencies. She felt a struggle. Must've been Steensen trying her best to feign a fight. Slaski was glad Steensen had allowed them in, had seen what she had seen.

Steensen yelped. Jarle laying another one on her for good effect no doubt. She fell, and soon Slaski was looking at Steensen's helmet jammed in the opposite footwell at the cusp of her vision. She heard the dull rip of tape through her helmet's pick-ups.

The door hatch opened.

The wind yowled.

The door hatch closed.

Jarle was gone.

Real food this time. Sort of. Slaski was glad it hadn't come out of a packet. Well, one she'd not seen anyway. And beer too, an ice cold one. One of many to come she hoped. She shovelled in another spoonful of stew and smiled as she looked up at Steensen, she looked good in Vasi light. Steensen finished the lump of bread she was chewing, washing it down with a swig of beer. Her eyes fixed on Slaski.

'We did the right thing,' Steensen said in an almost

inaudible tone. Not that she had to, they were the only ones in the canteen, most people were on clean up. Those that weren't were busy buzzing around R&D; the secret of inexium was out. Slaski and Steensen couldn't have asked for a better distraction.

Slaski took a long draft of beer.

'Yup. They—we—have double the chance now,' said Slaski.

'It still feels odd, all those voices. I can feel him too—Jarle. Something transferred,' said Steensen.

'They said that would pass, that it would all blend eventually.'

'I don't want it to.' Steensen's eyes faltered. Slaski put her bottle down, placed her right hand on Steensen's. Her eyes flickered up to meet Slaski's.

'Don't worry,' said Slaski, 'we just get away from here and the rest will take care of itself.'

They both straightened as the tannoy blared in the canteen. 'Second shuttle, ready for boarding. All rostered personnel report to pad A immediately.'

Slaski pushed her chair back from the table and stood, Steensen too, in the exact same manner. They both laughed then stooped to grab their carry-on bags, ensuring they didn't mirror each other this time and left the empty canteen to board their shuttle to the stars.

SILVER GHOSTS

Kristen failed to recall the last time he'd witnessed a soul quite like this. Another lifeforce. Not so close, anyhow. In and out of existence, fluttering in the red night like a faulty holo image. A dragon spirit of light. He dared not move, nor breathe too deeply. Afraid that venting gases from his EVA suit's breathing gear would disperse the spirit as it encircled him.

Knee deep in the dune he stood, motionless. The Ghost—what the team had nicknamed them—whipped up a whirlwind of sand around him and came so close he could almost hear its energy, as though it spoke through light. Even its armour—he imagined clacketing, rattling bone plates in life—spoke with static hisses and crackling intonation. Was this its grave?

Was he knee deep in its sand?

He considered digging, ploughing gloved hands

into fine grains, certain he would discover the long empty carapace the creature had left behind. It moans as if reading his thoughts.

Flickering spectral lights, blue-white in the dim burn of a red dwarf star. They cast a creeping shadow, a stretched-out figure across shifting sands. It burned now—core white. Its song in his head, calling to him.

My suit! My god, my suit.

Kristen had muted the sensor alerts as soon as he'd spotted the first glimmer coming over the dunes. Not wishing to enrage it—the team had already learnt the hard way.

The ghosts attacked noise.

Already legions, charred whiplash curls, threaded his suit's Exo-armour. Another minute and he would be toast.

So beautiful. Just a little longer. Just a few more—

'What makes you think they're alive?' Deacon's voice, petulant and condescending.

'Like I said, I don't think they're alive. Not in the common sense.' I tried to sound like I wasn't losing my patience, like he wasn't getting to me again. He was an engineer, what would he know about such things?

'Yeah, yeah.' He was dismissive, miming yapping mouths with his hands. He didn't even want to hear me out. But what else was there to do when stuck in a pod this small? The ghosts had damaged the other hab-modules. Whether it was an intended attack or simply a clumsy mistake was unknown, would never be known.

'But you think they *were* alive. Right? Dead, but still aware—sentient? You both thought that, you and Kristen.' He sounded sardonic in his inflection. Was he even aware of the mockery in his voice?

I looked out of the habitat's thick window, a 30 cm^2 quartz eye gazing out over the planes. The O_2 scrubbers filled in for the sound of desert wind, but they were rhythmic and regular, it was absurd. Everything was red out there and in here. We had cut all non-essential drains on power weeks ago.

Red.

It was as though there had only ever been one colour in the universe, and in how many tones? How many countless shades of the colour red could one possibly conjure up?

I had heard, as a child, that there was once a people that had three hundred words for snow and I wondered if anyone could think of as many for the colour red.

'Sam? Well? Are you even listening?'

It's hard to ignore someone in a twenty-metre-squared emergency habitation pod. And with only one window, the only thing close to televised entertainment, made it even harder to avoid them.

'Look, if you're not even going to engage, you might as well just—'

Don't finish that sentence. Just don't.

It was easy to hate in such confines. When the other person is so close they are almost inside you, wearing your skin.

You could wear *them*—the ghosts.

Like a spectral cloak, ethereal blue light. Crystal echoes of bone. Laser-light traces of a once living creature. An exoskeleton of energy.

But not for long. Not before they—

'Sam! For God's sake, will you just talk to me?' His face is red, but it's not the light. My silence is killing him. It's terrible I know, but I enjoy it, the power. The only entertainment besides that one-channel window. I turned from the window, from the desert. Back in the hab-pod now, the scrubbers blowing, Deacon blowing too.

'How much?' I asked.

'What?'

'Time. Since Clarke jury-rigged the antennae. Since he—'

Deacon shuffled across the cramped interior of the hab-pod. Foil wrappers of long dead meals, empty med-cartons and scattered water piping rustled at his ankles. He slumped over the white glowering screen of the console.

'Half an hour. Shit. Half an hour.'

Is that all?

It seemed like an eon since Clarke had suited up and fixed the antennae array. Before Deacon had been forced to follow after him—to dig his shallow grave next to Kristen's.

Deacon's face had changed, his thoughts carving out a new expression. Gone was the antagonism of boredom, death had stolen it.

'Looks like we're done then,' he said, resigned.

I said nothing. Just stared.

'God damn it Sam. Aren't you going to say anything?' Desperate now. Wavering.

'I tried to before.'

'Before?' Confusion. 'Oh Jesus, you mean—'

We both looked out at the swirling sand, mounds almost swallowed whole.

'I tried.' The tears won't come.

'Well damn you for not trying harder Sam. Damn you.' He didn't mean it. I know he didn't, not really.

I cast him a sharp glare anyway. His eyes darted back to the screen, then around the hab. Looking for food perhaps? Water? Some we had forgotten about.

'Check the reclaimer.'

'What?' He sounded agitated again. The fear dissolving away.

'For water. We've already drunk what we had before. So check the reclaimer.'

Deacon shuffled through the debris strewn across the hab, ankle deep in our own rubbish and filth. It stank, God knows it stank. But what else could we do with the toilets in the damaged pod? Going outside, that was—

'Nothing much.' Deacon sounded flat, rather than disappointed. 'So? *Do* you think they were alive once? Were the same as the things we found? Under the sand.'

Under the sand, next to Kristen's body. Deacon sounded like a child now. The lack of water suddenly robbing him of any malevolence or anger within. A weak, hungry, thirsty child.

I turned back to the red window. Such a huge universe confined within such a tiny circle. An untouchable world. Untastable. Never could we breathe this place, nor truly scoop the fine sand in bare hands. Never gaze upon the red light of the dwarf with naked eyes and feel the solar winds like *they* did. Do they still feel?

How does a ghost see the world? Does it perceive sound in colours? Vibrations in tones and hues? Do smells bloom in clouds of light or do they simply go unnoticed? I wondered how it would be to not have these senses at all, but to possess an entirely different set. A perspective so alien I would never comprehend.

Outside, the wind continued to swirl dervishes of sand into the air, uncovering now.

Clearing.

'Why'd you have to bury them so close Dee? Why'd you do that?'

Deacon collapsed into the junk with the weight of the memory and the hollow weakness two weeks without food brings.

'Ah, shit Sammi. Why'd you have to bring that up?'

His hands were still digging. Pulling away the fine grains. His back aching under the pressure of the damn planet. His heavy suit and the weight of his dead crewmates, Scarlet, Clarke and Kristen. The constant head twitches and jerking spasms of fear every time a glint of light, other than red, bent across his visor.

'It's just that the wind's uncovering them already. I can see his shoulder Dee. I can see Kristen's shoulder.'

The black lace legions were clear, even in the half light of the red night.

And something else. A sparkle? A glimmer?

No, it couldn't be.

'I'm not going back out,' Deacon said, trembling the words into existence. 'No chance in hell, Sam.

You can't make me.' He withdrew into the trash, disappearing amidst the remnants of our once civilised hab-pod. I had a hamster as a kid, did the same thing, bundled in junk, food, its own faeces. It had seemed happy though, content. Not like Deacon.

'They'll be back again. The hab's above their place. This is their sand.'

I watched as more of Kristen's Exo-armour slowly became exposed by the wind chasing away fine tracings of sand, sketching his body into the red world.

A drone.

The deep reverberations of a thousand Buddhist monks in prayer.

'You hear that?' The voice came from Deacon's pile. His refuse hideaway. Like a little boy in his den, frightened of the boogie man outside his bedroom door. Beyond the red window.

I nod.

Yes, I hear it. Damn it, I can feel it.

It was a deep lung rattling sound, creeping into the diaphragm, a resonating chamber of fear.

Now it was silver-blue inside the hab.

They're back.

'Oh Christ. Oh Christ.' Deacon wasn't praying. Any mention of God, His son or otherwise, was merely happenstance. A turn of phrase. No piety. Deacon didn't believe in that sort of thing.

'Shut up,' I whispered, trying not to make too much noise.

Bluish-crystal light frosted the glass pane by my face and I could feel its energy. Actually *feel* it.

Serpentine their shape, an electric glow of ethereal energies. You could almost feel the soul buzz of their life, lingering light patterns, feelings etched into the molecules of air. Their shape matched that of the fossils in the sand, perfect millipede creatures preserved in eons of dust. That was how Kristen had made the connection, after the first attack. After he had found Scarlet dead.

Tendril clusters, a trillion hair-like legs, burned bright lightning strikes of ghostly thread.

'Are they still there?'

'Shut up,' I said, as if I were a trained ventriloquist, hardly moving my lips. The light fixed there and I swallowed dryly. *Not yet. Damn you. Not yet.* If I was to die, it would be on my own terms. Not cowered in fear, screaming.

The humming dulled, the light diminished.

Deacon's sigh was louder than the scrubbers.

'They're gone?' he asked in a whimper.

I nodded. Daring not to make a noise to bring them back. As much as they fed off fear, certain sounds drew them, movement too. But they were long gone, out there in the desert again. Maybe they know we are dead anyway.

It's just a matter of time.

'Two hours,' said Deacon.

'Then do it.' My voice was cold.

Deacon emerged from his pile and was at the console faster than I had seen him move in a long time. A flurry of clacketing on the keyboard and the affirmative beep confirmed the distress call had been sent. We'd managed enough of a charge then. If only the cells had charged earlier, two or three hours. Perhaps we'd have gotten a message out in time. This call for help though, well, it was nothing more than two ghosts shrieking out into the night.

'That's that.'

He slumped on the spot, on his knees in the trash, staring at the screen. I turned back to the red window. Kristen's body fully exposed now like some great Pharaoh of Earth. Black legions clear, charred worms lacing his suit.

Another glimmer.

What is *that?*

Deacon spoke, his voice startlingly loud in the absence of worldly sounds other than the scrubbers. He didn't move. Didn't want to face me. 'Think they'll get the signal before—'

'—probably not,' I said. I glanced back outside, searching for that evasive light. The clean light. 'I'm going to suit up.'

'What?' Deacon cocked his head in alarm. But still didn't turn. Not bodily.

'I'm ready. I'm going out. I know a place somewhere.' A rocky formation where I could die with a view—alone. But then, perhaps not die at all, not really.

He turned his face to the screen again, backlit in the white light of it, his silhouette was a ghostly black emptiness. 'You'll die for sure… Just like the others. You know that, right?' No emotion in his voice anymore, not even a trace of anger.

'We all die Deacon,' I said and stared long at the shimmering human form slowly being unveiled by the wind, 'but only some of us get the chance to live again.'

'What?'

I chose not to answer him. He wouldn't have understood even if I had explained what I had figured out. I stood up. The ache of effort an unwelcome reunion with pain. Sliding the heavy Exo-suit on was a torture. I was glad that ended with the final struggle of lifting that helmet on and cinching it shut. Deacon never offered to help. He had just remained there, on his knees.

Maybe he had found a god right there in the computer screen. In the white light.

Or maybe it was the hope sheer willpower would bring rescue. Perhaps he would stare at the screen so hard, force a response to appear. *But he must know. He must. It's too late for us that way.*

'I'll see you then,' I said. What I meant to say was *I'm sorry.* It didn't come out.

'Damn you Sammi. Damn you for bringing us here.' It was meant to be a simple geological survey, that's all. No one expected to find fossils, especially not ghosts.

The airlock hisses, opens and closes and I am outside.

The hab looks so insignificant from out here. Out in the desert. Redness forever tinging everything. I turned to Kristen, his silver-light body there, right there. I wondered if Deacon was even watching, if he could see this.

Threads of light, ethereal silver-blue. Neon light in the red night. Kristen was comprised of them alone. No suit. There was no need. They had brought him back, the essence of him at least. Together, entwined in the ghost's essence, perhaps humans could live on this rock after all. It was just a case of letting go of that to which we clung so fiercely.

I could have told Deacon. But for what?

Instead I embraced Kristen. His hands leaving blackening legions all over my suit. For a moment, doubt came to me again, but soon departed, there in Kristen's arms of silver energy. These things, these ghosts were trying to help us. Help us evolve, become them. To be released from the burdens our technology brings and the false concept of ourselves. We are so much more than just tissue. I was certain in that moment, I would return. A silver ghost in the red night.

FEEDING THE GODS

Blue-green phosphorescent limbs of living particles ascended on the warm evening air. Vaporous fingers challenging the world. Oscillating from nooks of orange rust dusted trees like probing hands. Ethereal eddies coiling from the undersides of ferns, streamers of sapphire smoke peeling away from the slumped heads of doleful bluebells. The forest was truly alive and probably held more life now than it ever had boasted before.

Kayden admired all of it as Sol dissolved into the thinning golden line of the horizon. The first of them, the blue-green spore, minute things in their billions, would soon descend once more to seek bodily warmth like gnats tracing hot mammal breath. They would tickle his shaven head and exposed hands, those parts not protected beneath golden-brown robes.

Cross-legged on a mossy spot within the creeping

fringe of the darkling forest, Kayden was confident in his safety with an ancient lunging oak at his back. Its trunk elephantine and swollen, spore-sick. Most things were spore-sick now.

Except him.

He had picked out the spot just as Sol had begun its long bow to the night, a safe place to meet the spore swarms with a tranquil, emancipated mind.

These days, the forests carpeting Britain were darkest before the dusk. They inched their growth each day, unrestrained by human hands. The ember glow of smouldering lights, towns and cities had long been snuffed. Nature had begun its siege, the old places were already beginning to yield, giving over to the dominion of every growing green thing.

Even the summer moon and stars seemed at odds against the spore clouds. Unable to show themselves at this darkest of moments where one could feel utterly alone in the world. Even more so since most of the human population had descended into spore-sleep leaving the lucky few to the engulfing embrace of solitude.

Kayden and solitude were old comrades.

Since he was nineteen, he had spent his life in isolation cubes and even out in the salty air, the Isle of Silence had been forever a place where only the singularly devoted dared brave such remoteness. Little had he known then how his time spent on that frozen Shetland island would prepare him for the new world.

The north, such a frigid bleak place, even before Britain had plunged into darkness. That treeless isle, where even lichen and moss seemed haggard and sought shelter burying themselves in napes and clinging to nooks in jutting limestone islands. Grey-green sentinels standing defiant against the gale breaths of the North Sea.

There it had been cold.

But here, in this forest, Kayden felt an earthy warmth. He often ruminated on the price paid for that warmth—the price others had paid. In that dark moment he pondered for the last time that day as he hunkered down his mind for the night's watch. The now silver threaded horizon, dappling beyond the trees, winked out like a gasping flame clinging to a dwindling candle wick.

The forest sank into a light where colour seemed bleached from the world and in that chrome realm the blue-green spore grew brighter and breathed with Kayden in pulsing luminosity, emboldened by Sol's absence. Drawing close on his in-breath, diminishing with each out-breath, the spore flowed. Kayden took no heed of the tiny invaders, these miniscule genetic tinkerers. Nor would he entertain his thoughts, not until the dawning liquid gold of Sol kissed his skin again.

Thinking was a daylight indulgence.

Bird song ceased abruptly, as it had done since *their* arrival and in the same instant the forest, so hushed and shadowy at dusk, ignited with a living bioluminescent flourish. Life not quite earthly, yet not wholly alien. The spores' doing, those dabblers, those biomolecular manipulators.

Leaves fluttered like finches ruffling their feathers. Branches stretched out the aches of the day like fatigued labourers. Mosses quivered as if taken by a sudden chill and ferns cast spells quivering like an illusionist's magical fingers.

Taking in a voluminous draught of forest air through a prominent nose, Kayden allowed his lids to settle together beneath a strong hairless brow against the spore glow, against the architects of New Britain. For some reason or other—Kayden had his theories—the spore would not affect him, even when inhaled. They would simply exit like hoary breath on an icy day.

He had witnessed the spore for the first time not long after stepping off the drone boat on his return to the mainland after many years in silent retreat and they had lingered ever since. As darkness fell, so did they fall upon the conscious. As coolness stole warmth from the day, so too did they rob the warmth from the living. Ensuring he remained purged of craving shelter and comfort, free of aversion towards the spore, Kayden breathed.

Most would need to reign in the agony of losing everyone, governing the dread of true isolation, the insidious anxiety of a person pursued, Kayden simply breathed.

He had witnessed the spore gorge on fear like a

cloud of famished mosquitos. Witnessed some of his brothers taken into a sleep from which they never awoke.

A soft push of evening air, and with it the scent of juniper, reminded him to maintain a motionless mind and posture. To focus solely on the physical sensations his seated position on the mossy floor brought him.

Legs burned from running. Shoulders ached in memory of flight. His neck, weary of casting nervous glances behind. He noted tension in his jaw, released it along with the subtle frown which had seized his brow. He permitted sensations to shift and play as they would, free from the cataloguing habits of the mind.

The swarm persisted to billow about him, he could feel it. They would never sleep, not at night, so neither would he. In sleep his mind might wander, slip into a dream or subconscious thought and they would have him.

There was no need to dwell on those that followed him at least. Those he hoped he had lost. Had it been a day? Two days head start on them? He felt the spore haze tremor at the thought and immediately set it free.

Sleep, like thinking, was done in daylight— provided one could find somewhere safe. Kayden wasn't the only survivor though and not all kept as peaceful a mind as he. Dwelling in disused mines, sewers and deep stinking wet caves where the spore seemed not to venture. Most had become desperately mad, savage creatures. It dismayed him how humanity had descended so readily.

The blue-green spore preferred airy, dark, dry places. With an appetite for thoughts it entered through the pores, melting like snowflakes on warm skin, seeking consciousness. That was how they took you under, into spore sleep. At least, that was how they had taken swathes of the population on the first day. Kayden knew nothing of the fate of the world at large.

It had taken all life in fact, flora and fauna. Yet such life reacted differently. Spore had swollen the skin of trees, painted the whole country with colourful rusty, flaky growths as though a child had tossed powder paint around in a gleeful dance. Some creatures evaded mutation, just as the feral humans, in shaded dank nests.

Something stirred deep within the subtler layers of mind. A thought so strong it took skill to preserve the balance he had cultivated. The swarm shivered. Something was observing him, some transmuted woodland creature perhaps? The followers? Had they discovered him?

Reeling his attention in as would a fisherman acutely aware of an overburdened line, Kayden eased his mind ashore until it lay mollified at his feet and he dug in for the night. Whatever or whoever was scrutinizing him would have to delay their intentions until morning, if they were so inclined to waiting.

*

Dawn came somewhat sooner than Kayden had anticipated. The first bird to brave a call had confused him. He imagined the creature had made some error, awoken too early and in celebration of the absence of humans let slip an eager note. When he felt the warming fingers of Sol walking across his bald pate, he knew the bird had made no mistake.

The spore had retreated to its various hiding places as soon as daylight had begun to eat away the night. The forest had ceased its glow and now only the muted colours of spore rust remained, bereft of its otherworldly radiance. Sleep seemed but a memory to Kayden, the desire for it a long-forgotten custom of the old world.

Remaining there a little longer he sat, long skinny legs knotted on the mossy forest floor, the morning light breaking through the speckled canopy of indigo tinged ash and vermilion splashed oak kissing warm spots here and there warming the robes draped on his thinning physique, a frame in want of more frequent sustenance.

He breathed in the rich aromatic scent of sulphur dusted liverwort and the musty dampness of russet flecked fungi, imagining a limestone cave or crag nearby hairy with lichen. A moist cave, perfect for those who trailed him. He felt it again then; the patient presence. Almost lost on the concentrative watches of the night was the awareness of it, daylight now wrought the threat fresh to a mind open to contemplation, to concern, to lingering anxieties.

'How do you do it?' The subdued raspy voice told of a hard life. The speaker pressed the question once more. 'How?'

As light as the words she spoke she glided along the forest floor toward him, like a breeze herself. Kayden was certain the presence was female and that she was not one of those who followed. The followers never spoke, not words he understood anyway. They certainly never asked questions.

'Do what?' asked Kayden in an amused, approachable manner as the prickly memory of the followers dissolved. Before her came the attitude of a skittish deer. Kayden elected to keep his eyes closed and remain tranquilly immobile for fear of alarming her. Peaceful creatures were hard to come by nowadays and the potential of company was a novelty he was happy to entertain.

'They don't put you to sleep. Don't change you. Why?' asked the woman with the plain speech of someone not acquainted to the usual and expected conversational preamble. She was a little closer now. She is crouched, thought Kayden as he heard the moss and twigs giving under her efforts.

'Is it because you're a monk?'

Kayden smiled. 'No. *They* take monks too.'

'Really?' She sounded as though she thought him a liar. He could forgive her for the mistake. No doubt she had seen him sitting through the night and attributed his skills to all such *Satva* monks as him, which led him to question her.

'I'm curious too,' said Kayden, eyelids still lightly pressed together and with a smile he hoped would dissolve her trepidation. 'How do *you* do it?'

'Do what?'

'Remain untaken. You're the first I've come across in a *very* long time,' he didn't count the followers, they weren't really human anymore, 'I find a lot of sleepers.' He wrestled his mind from to those who followed.

'Oh, I think it's me hat,' she told him thoughtfully. Curiosity had snared Kayden now, and after a couple measured breaths, he cracked his eyes, allowing the tangerine light seen through skin and blood vessels to bleed ochre then white.

The forest painted itself across the bleached canvas of his vision brushing in shapes of swollen oaks and fissured trunks of mature ash scattered here and there along with slender birch and shaggy elder. Already, colourful tinkered insects were on the wing enjoying the warmth of Sol. He thought of the damp cave nearby, thought of the followers. Had they been there they would be on them both by now he believed. That they were not, eased the tension which had set his shoulders like granite blocks.

The spindly young woman, perhaps in her twenties, though she seemed aged by a harsh existence, sat directly in front of him, the foil hat she had referred to glinting in the morning light like crushed glass. It was crumpled and crafted into a pudding bowl shape, the crown tapering into a point which gave Kayden the impression of an acorn cupule. From under its uneven rim caerulean eyes, like a summer sky, observed him intensely. To be looked upon in such a way by the unordained was no novelty, yet he sensed something singular in the manner in which she observed him. It was the look of an initiate prior to ordination—potentiality.

Matted auburn hair sprang out unruly and tangled resting against freckled skin like swirling twiggy bird nests. He caught the sour scent of sweat along with the usual forest smells of leaf rot and damp moss and wondered how he smelt to her. As rare as a hot bath, he thought.

'Nice hat,' he told her, and he truly meant it as, in a strange way, it suited her. 'I would never have thought—'

'—I've always had it,' said the young woman with wary enthusiasm. A soft smile sketched her eyes into crescents. 'Even before the blue stuff came. People said I was crazy. But who's crazy now, hey?'

Her lips crept into a manic grin. She uncrossed and crossed her rangy legs, attempting to mimic him, not quite managing to get comfy. 'How can you sit like that?' She pulled a puzzled expression that looked as though she were on the brink of a sneeze.

Kayden shrugged. 'Years of practice.'

The young woman barked out an awkward laugh and shifted uneasily, eyes flickering about like a cornered forest creature searching for an escape should the need arise. She seemed more like a child than and adult, still becoming accustomed to her presence in the world. She'd been alone a long time, thought Kayden, even before they came.

'Me too. Practice I mean...' she said just barely snagging the last thread of conversation before the opportunity had completely expired. 'Since I left school. Me mom kicked me out. Called me a no-good loser. Been sitting on the street ever since. But I didn't care none, I managed to find places to get high. You ever been high? I suppose not, being a monk an' all.'

'I wasn't always a monk,' said Kayden with a soft smile the implication of which he thought she would take however she chose to take it. She appeared to approve of the remark, eyes glowering, lips trembling with too many budding words, brain not knowing which to voice first. He was probably the first person she had seen in a good long while. She had a thirsty eagerness to her.

'You a special one?'

The question threw him. 'Huh?'

The young woman waved her hand around the top of her head, over the tinfoil hat. 'The thing there, those marks. That a tattoo, or what? Didn't think monks got tattoos.'

She meant the mandala which capped his skull down to his hairless brow. Kayden always forgot it was there. The mark of his ascension. 'This? Ha, well, yes. Some monks have them.'

'That's what does it, right? What keeps 'em away?'

'No, it's just ink. No kind of mark can protect against spore. I block them, like your hat.' He supposed that wasn't entirely true, failing to see how baking foil would have any effect against the spore.

The young woman cocked her head as if catching a whisper with small buttercup ears then sprang up to approach him. He permitted her to run her fingers over his smooth scalp, examining it. Her touch was tender even though her hands were coarse.

'Did it hurt?'

'The tattoo? Aye, you bet,' said Kayden. The young woman laughed then backed off, reclaiming her seat on spongey spore-sick moss that now looked more akin to brain coral. She put her knees up by her ears and arms around her legs, fingers knitted.

'I'm Kayden.' He pressed his hands together in blessing.

'Riley,' she said, pressing her own hands together in delighted amusement at the sharing of such a gesture.

Kayden grinned and thought of how he was taking a liking to this young soul. 'Riley, hey?' The name triggered some trivia from his childhood reading. 'Did you know your name means brave?'

Riley snorted, tilting backwards as if the hilarity of the remark had slapped her like a stout gust of wind.

'No. Ha. I definitely ain't. All I've ever done is run away from this and that. Only reason I'm off the gear is because of *them*. No one around selling no more.' She chortled again and said, 'Suppose I should be grateful to 'em. You're Kaleb, right?'

'Kayden.'

'Right. Whatsit mean?'

'It means steadfast,' he said, shifting his posture to allow his feet to wake up, the flow of blood a tingling fire of life. Riley pulled another face, baffled. 'Steadfast,' he said again, 'you know... faithful.'

She formed a wide O with her mouth and nodded. 'Riiight. Gotchya. Well, ain't we a pair? Brave and steadfast.'

Kayden nodded, then eased himself to his feet, swept up his golden-brown shoulder bag and flung it over his head so the strap lay diagonal across his chest almost disappearing in his tan robes. He dusted off what spore rust clung to them.

'You're going?' Riley's voice caught in her throat. She stood and padded around the moss fretfully, acting every bit the distressed deer again.

'You can follow if you wish,' said Kayden. You should follow, he willed her. She need not know what stalked him. She perked up at the suggestion, stiff and straight like an excited child.

'Where are we going?' asked Riley, as Kayden ambled along.

'South.'

'I came from that way, from Lancaster. There's nothing there but...' Riley came to a standstill with a black look about her as though she were driving back something dark and dreadful. 'Why South?' she asked, correcting her foil hat with minute tentative adjustments.

'I came from the North—the Shetlands.'

'Woah. Scotland? You walked *all* that way? Why?'

Kayden paused and twisted to look at her, his expression bemused. 'Nothing much else *to* do,' he told her, returning his attention to the footpath which curved to the left where the rainbow dusted trees thinned. Beyond stretched rolling fells, a patchwork quilt of colour. He heard Riley pick up her feet and continue along with him. 'Besides,' he said. 'It's warmer down South.'

'But they like the warm.'

'So do I,' said Kayden, turning to flash a smile.

As they walked, Kayden recalled childhood trips with his father to the South where the sand was gold not grey and the sea was blue and not grey either. Not like the Silent Isle. The South seemed a healthier place in which to dwell in such spare times. Any slight benefit outweighed the negatives. Warm weather was certainly preferable to the alternative and winter was on its way. At first, the frigid North had been more of a refuge. Lower levels of spore meant a life freer of spore threat. However, what pockets of humanity that had survived up there had soon turned sour once food supplies dwindled.

Living off the land was no option. Most things were spore-sick, tainted. Once the stores, houses and anywhere in which preserved food could be found had dried up, that's when folk turned on each other. Kayden had left that madness, ironically running into the exact same climate which ensured higher spore levels, which in turn meant less humans.

They hiked a while, mostly in swift silent steps on his part, yet the day was far from quiet. Diamond flecked blackbirds and flower-petaled blue tits intoned their spirited songs and Kayden was convinced he had heard the shrill throaty call of a peregrine somewhere above, obscured by the glare of Sol.

Occasionally Kayden would answer some question or other, usually about the Silent Isle and its isolation cubes. Riley was curious and each answer saw her descend deeply into a philosophical daze. She made no mention of their swift pace and Kayden sought not to raise the topic. Instead, he casually glanced over his shoulder now and then, searching for gloomy shapes against the variegated hills.

The town traced one edge of the lake, sprawled out, hidden by the encroaching forest here and there, all nestled within the fells. The view from the hill they stood atop was enough to confirm the place was bereft of human activity.

'You're actually going down there?' said Riley, standing a few feet back from Kayden as if being any closer would commit her to his idea. 'They are down there you know. They're always in places like that. It's the houses.'

'I know. But it's still light,' said Kayden, squinting up at Sol burning in the big blue.

'Yeaahh, but...' argued Riley, searching for excuses but finding none. She moved back a step. 'Ain't you afraid? Don't you hate 'em?'

'Afraid? No,' said Kayden gently. 'As for hate... What's to hate? After all, the spore is life, like everything else.'

'They just consume everything though,' she argued, 'take it over, make it suit them. Everything they touch they change.'

'Not everything,' said Kayden, gesturing the both of them. 'Besides,' he glanced down at the town, 'isn't that what we have done? This planet, this place... all of it,' he turned and held her gaze, 'was changed long before they arrived. We were on the verge of destruction at our own hands. If anything—'

'—don't say they saved the planet,' Riley snapped, 'don't say that!'

Kayden could see there was no arguing it. She hated the spore and his indifference seemed to anger her. He remained silent for a moment, allowing the breeze to carry the mood along with it.

Kayden patted his shoulder bag. 'We need food, water...' Riley's eyes were still narrowed in consideration of his previous words yet she said nothing. Kayden rubbed the fine haze of stubble on his head. 'Razors perhaps. There's bound to be something. Although, it's hard to really tell from this distance. We'll know for sure when we get down there.'

It had been instant—*the Plunge*. Kayden, despite having been on the Isle of Sorcha, had managed to piece together events from what he had seen and the few survivors he had met along the way—and the sleepers.

He had actually seen the deep space freighter come burning into Earth's atmosphere like a comet, though hadn't known what it was at the time. Then it was too late, the world plunged into a deep sleep as the spore wave hit, not that he could have done much about it.

'What's it mean?' asked Riley, in that way she had about her. The curiosity of a child tinged with the calculated agenda of an adult. Kayden responded with what had become one of his stock responses to her questions as they hiked, 'What's what mean?'

'Spore. Back in the forest this morning. You said, "ink can't protect against spore", or somethin' like that and I was wonderin' what it meant but couldn't figure it meself. So, tell me...'

They both stood there like clothed statues, the fabric of their garments flapping in the rising gusts coming up the gentle slope of the fell as Kayden explained.

She seemed oblivious to the news that a star ship had crashed to Earth so many months ago, the devastation it had brought to the South. The impact had sent a tsunami wiping most of Cornwall clean. It was what intrigued him about the South; a clean slate. That much Kayden had gleaned from scraps of hearsay as he had journeyed down from the Shetlands (news updates were rarely received on Sorcha).

There had been three of them in the beginning. Brothers Dorn and Sonne. What happened to Sonne was how they learned of the spore. They had found a sleeper in the street and mistaken the poor woman to be afflicted with some disease and were astonished that she had been left unattended, so carried her into an abandoned cottage to care for her whilst they figured out where everybody had gone.

It wasn't until the evening, when the light-sensitive spore had poured from her ears and nose like blue shimmering smoke and took Sonne that they became aware of the danger. Sonne, whose depth and understanding of the subtle layers of mind was still in its infancy.

It had been Kayden's turn to meditate and Dorn's to watch over their comatose brother the following night. Dorn reported the spore spiralling around them both in columns like a hesitant and frustrated school of fish. They speculated that it was their practice of mental discipline that had protected them.

'What happened to the other guy?' asked Riley, in a

matter-of-fact manner that wasn't entirely unfeeling.

'Dorn?' said Kayden. 'He fell as we descended the Highlands. Broke his ankle. We had no medical supplies and rations were low. It got infected... it spread. I stayed with him until the end,' Kayden told her without a trace of anguish.

'Did you cry?' asked Riley, again, Kayden sensed no intended discourtesy. He cracked a smile. He admired Riley's unattachment to convention, her questioning mind. 'No.' He looked out over the town below.

'Do monks not cry? Don't you care?'

He turned unhurriedly to face her again and explained what had been expounded to him in the early days after he had taken refuge in the Brotherhood of None.

The information was intellectually understood he surmised. She seemed familiar with letting go, non-attachment, even equanimity. He considered whether she actually needed that foil hat of hers or not.

Gingerly, Riley trailed Kayden down the rough, craggy path of stones to a drystone wall where pastel pink and blue lichen seemed the dominant lifeform. They clambered over the old unsteady stile there and once on the other side felt cool air wafting off the lake in uplifting waves.

He regarded the National Trust signpost upright next to the stile which indicated the town was indeed Windermere, as he had anticipated, and that it lay one kilometre down the road they were about to step onto.

'We're really going in there? Don't you fear them? You really don't hate them?' asked Riley again, as though she were testing his resolve. She stood with one hand on the stile as though it were her anchor to safety.

There was no need for her to hesitate. She had seen the swarm around him, as Dorn had. If you had memories of spore swarms, then you would be fine. That much he had learned on his travels.

A screech stole his attention but for a second and he spoke half attentive to his words, half intent on the sound. 'No. As I told you, I don't fear or hate them. Come, trust in your hat.'

He struck off down the road wondering exactly what the noise had been and found himself wanting shelter. Somewhere safe, somewhere secure.

Spaghetti Hoops, baked beans and chilli con carne. Can after can. Riley filled her tattered old pack. 'Flippin' heck. This town was hit bad. They didn't even have time to knock over the shops. What's this?' She held up a slab of something in vacuum sealed white plastic.

Kayden looked up from the shelf of Pasta 'n' Sauces he was raiding. 'It's mint cake.'

She sniffed the plastic wrapper. 'Is it good?'

'Awful,' said Kayden. 'But don't let me stop you. Make up your own mind.' Riley hesitated, put it in, took it out, read the label, then finally settled on it placing in her bag. 'So much sugar.' She grinned yellow teeth.

Kayden nodded, looked left and right, spied what he was after and grabbed the items flinging them to Riley who caught them with startling alacrity. She eyed the toothpaste and toothbrush with incredulity. 'What you sayin? Me breath stinks or summit?'

'I'm merely encouraging good oral hygiene,' he said and flaunted immaculate teeth. 'It's the end of the world, sister. Two things you need to take care of: teeth and feet.'

He glanced at her trainers that screamed for retirement, then his own dilapidated pair, checking the worn soles. 'We need new footwear. This is a tourist town, there will be something somewhere.'

Riley perked up a little. 'Shopping?' She looked at her grimy old tracksuit top and grease spotted jeans, then at Kayden. 'What about you. Gonna ditch the blanket?'

'Robes,' he said with measured patience and a slight chuckle. 'They're robes, and no. Although, I would like to find a new sleeping bag and some thermals. Maybe some socks too.'

Winter would be with them soon enough, something they were both painfully aware of. Kayden appreciated how being in this town, right now, was certainly auspicious. Here he could stock up, maybe even wait out those who followed. Weather that storm. Perhaps they would pass through like the locusts they were and leave Riley and him alone.

As a child, his father had encouraged preparedness. A military man, fond of camping and survival. It had made for an enjoyable childhood. Kayden had cherished the trips to the highlands and forests when his father was on leave. The adventure, the advice, the seclusion. Perhaps one of the reasons he had taken refuge. The isolation. Donning the brown robes of a monk instead of the green fatigues of a soldier had seemed the right course to take at the time. That his father had been killed in action had sealed the decision.

They gathered as much food and water as they could comfortably carry with a few extra Bags for Life. Kayden imagined he would *actually* keep them for life too, however long that would be.

Riley had glanced at him a few times and Kayden worried she had recognised the apprehension in his eyes, somehow penetrating the relaxed mask he wore. At one moment her lips had motioned as though to form another question, perhaps the question he feared, but nothing came of it. He was glad at that. She didn't need to know what possibly stalked them.

Windermere was a ghost town, like most British towns since the Plunge. Nature had begun its assault immediately after humans were put to sleep. Roofs had promptly given under summer rains, pavements and roads fractured and flaked under the coercion of weeds empowered by alien genes and, in some areas, flood water had swallowed streets back into bog and mire.

Riley had been correct in her assumptions. The town must have been hit at night, only a few people lay in the streets or slept in cars, still buckled in. All of them in that queer state of preservation spore sleep cast upon them. Untouched by microbes, birds and surviving mammals alike. Most untainted creatures, those which had managed to avoid the spore by their mere choice of habitation, kept away from sleepers. Perhaps they knew somehow, some animal instinct. Knew what would erupt from them when Sol dipped away and evening came.

It was a shame, Kayden would often reflect, that humanity had been so intent on commerce and amassing wealth that it had ignored the obvious warnings the planet had given them. After worldwide flooding had come civil unrest. Drinking water was in great want. Britain itself, now had long stretches of hot weather he'd never known as a child. Perfect for spore. Very little rain to provide respite.

At first, as they had wandered into the ghost town, Riley had seemed to find it odd that Kayden took the time to either hide sleepers under nearby cover or at least build a shelter from what he could find lying around for each one he couldn't move.

'Until they wake,' he said each time hoping Riley wouldn't pry any further. But covering them felt like the only decent thing to do, considering.

Every sleeper seemed well preserved, despite having been sleeping for countless months and Kayden painstakingly dusted the dirt off their faces as if each one were a sick brother or sister. Riley still couldn't bring herself to touch them no matter how much he demonstrated there was nothing to fear. She watched though; her head curiously cocked. Bemused he imagined.

The majority of townsfolk were housebound no doubt. Gaunt and ashen faced as the rest, very gradually deteriorating as the spore progressively drank up the nutrients from their bodies. But first, they always drank away your mind. It was a better way to go and sometimes, when his mind was weak, Kayden envied them. Ignorant in their sleep, unaware of what travelled the daylight hours over mountain and fell.

You were safe during the day so long as you weren't out in the open. Thinking wouldn't find you taken by the spore in daylight hours either, nevertheless, Kayden was always cautious of the mind slipping back into its old habits, even during the safer hours of daylight. He saw the days as time to practise a steadfast mind, ready for the marathon nights.

He likened night time thinking to sending a strong radio signal broadcasting, 'Hey, I'm here. Come get me.' At least that was how he expressed it to Riley as they looted an outdoors store for warm clothing ready for the coming winter.

Riley theorised on the magical properties of tin foil and tattoo ink as they selected new backpacks and perused camping equipment. At one point, Kayden had thought he had convinced her the answer was not external but internal. It was just unfortunate happenstance that she was convinced foil hats actually did anything, but again, did the root of her emancipation really matter? If it worked, it worked, right?

'What do you think?' said Riley, holding up a leaf-green windcheater. Kayden considered it with a thoughtful gaze. 'A suitable colour choice, lightweight and warm.'

Riley swung her head and rolled her eyes. 'Geez, loosen up monk. Does it look *good*?'

Kayden looked around the empty store and distinct lack of people, then to Riley again. 'Does it matter?'

She tied it around her waist and sighed. 'You're like a robot. You know that?' Kayden smiled and turned back to the thermal underwear he was perusing. He chose two sets of black.

A shriek brought them to stare at the shop entrance. The door stood ajar, the glass spiderwebbed but not completely broken through. It would take but a gentle push Kayden imagined. He felt his mouth suddenly parched, swallowing a great effort. He licked his lips and breathed, calming his deepest fears.

They had found him.

So soon? It saddened him to see Riley, an ashen ghost of herself. He should have told her to go when they first met, should have known better. Kayden looked around the store in desperation. The spore he could handle, but these followers. These stalkers...

There must be a something somewhere to sure up, block vents and gaps around doors. 'One minute,' he said and hurried past a staff-only sign to the rear of the store returning within seconds.

'This way. There's a storeroom,' he said as urgently as he could without causing more alarm. He scanned the shop and glimpsed what he was looking for, swept over to a shelf and snatched several first aid kits. He saw something better than medical tape then: packing tape by the till.

'Grab the packing tissue too,' he said, pointing to a pile of boots still waiting to be stuffed and boxed.

Riley did as he asked silently and they both sought shelter, plugging any gaps with tissue and packing tape, just in case sound should escape. Sound and scent.

'What was that scream?' whispered Riley, eyes fixed on their handy work about the door. 'Why are we in here?'

With a sigh, Kayden finally spoke what he had been so reluctant to say. She had asked him a direct question and he felt obliged to answer.

'I came across them a few days ago. I thought I had lost them.' He cursed himself for not being more vigilant. But there was no time for regret.

'At first I thought I had found a settlement. Spore survivors. I came upon a damp cave; the kind spore stays away from for whatever reason. I heard a cry.' He shook his head and glanced down at his crossed legs.

'I was a fool. I thought I could help them. But they are beyond help sister. Beyond reach.' His mind slid to that moment at the mouth of that cave. There again, standing over the remains of those the followers had already consumed and other sleepers stored close by.

'Killing the sleepers kills the spore,' he said plainly. 'It seems the spore needs life. The plants and animals continue on, changed but something of the animal remains,' he furrowed his brows, 'something about humans... Perhaps our brand of consciousness. I don't know. Whatever it is it causes the spore to put us to sleep.

'Their restorative powers can't work without the host continuing its customary habits of eating and drinking though.' Kayden stared at the door. 'If only some kind of mutual arrangement—' a shriek took the rest of his words.

Riley stared wide eyed as she drank in what he was saying. 'After those people,' Kayden continued in the silence that followed the screech, 'if they can be called people anymore, kill the sleepers, they...' he couldn't finish his sentence. Couldn't actually speak it. But there was no need. From her expression, he could tell Riley had got the message.

'That's why you hide them,' she said perceptively, nodding. 'You're protecting them?'

Kayden nodded. He sat then, in his nest of sleeping bags wondering if Riley would find it hard to sleep in such cramped confines with all the vents and gaps in the room blocked but she proved she was still full of surprises. It would do to get some sleep before night came. The ignorance sleep brought would serve as a shroud from the followers. He noted the chair he'd wedged against the handle of the door. Good and sturdy. It would have to do. He closed his eyes and surrendered to exhaustion.

Night came, spore too, through gaps so minuscule not even Kayden's tape and packing paper could block them out. Both he and Riley sat through the night in a state between consciousness in their own ways.

The next day passed hot and stuffy in their hideout. Outside, inhuman screams and primal shrieks had stolen the playful twitter of bird song. Where once a gentle breeze sighed, heavy scraping movements and the crash of glass reigned. One of them had come upon the stores. At that time the door handle had rattled wildly with their efforts to open it. Thankfully, whoever it was had most likely assumed the door locked, much to Kayden's relief. They had been lucky this time.

The following night came in blue-green shimmers as it had for so long now, only Kayden felt more at ease with the spore about. Assured that those creatures who had taken the day were in some dank sewer, somewhere too damp for spore to follow.

It was early the next morning when they finally elected to leave having eaten all of the food in their closet, even the mint cake. With judicious, measured movements they peeled back the tape, moved the chair and eased the door open. Each second Kayden willed the door to not squeak. Every sound seemed a cacophony capable of waking even the sleepers. His eyes were drawn immediately to the street and scanning for evidence of the monsters that had come for them.

Beyond the door, which still rested ajar, the day shined bright and birds sang. It was as if it were any other day. They both donned their newly acquired packs in slow considered motions and made toward the door. A glint caught Kayden's vison and he froze, his hand clutching at the sleeve of Riley's green windcheater. She looked at him askance as though he were mad. She meant to speak but he pressed a finger to his lips and upraised his hairless brow directing her gaze with his eyes. She tracked his line of sight and he saw her recognition. By her wide eyes, she knew what he knew.

The glass door had been destroyed; the shattered pane dusted the floor like frost across a wintry field catching morning light. They had laid a trap, Kayden considered that. What that evidenced... how much "human" remained in them? They had cast down the clothes rails and scattered the shelving too. Through the tangle of it his heart pounded as though he were running, despite them creeping slower than sloths.

By the time they made the street, Kayden felt as though he would never be able to still his mind again. They made their way out of town, checking their backs as they skulked along the cracked road and in his haste to tread soft soundless ground, Kayden found himself come to the same fate as Dorn had all those months ago.

They had passed the last of the houses a while back and Kayden was climbing over the stile opposite the one that had led them to the town. The wood was rotten and slick with morning moisture. Under Riley's sparrow weight, it had been fine, but Kayden proved too much for it.

The snap was loud enough. His scream too, as he came crashing down in a cloud of multicoloured dust on the road side of the drystone wall. He had that to be grateful for. Riley wouldn't have to heave him back over again. He cursed himself for being hasty all the same.

'They say most accidents happen within in a mile of home,' whispered Riley, still cautious of making any loud sounds as she splinted up Kayden's leg according to his directions.

'I'm pretty sure that fact is regarding driving,' he said, stifling back another cry of pain. Riley perceived his discomfort and rested for a minute before continuing to wrap the bandage around his leg.

'Well...' she said standing, rubbing her hands together. She appeared pleased with her field dressing.

'Good thing we've got enough first aid kits to stick a small army back together, ain't it?'

Kayden looked down at his leg, assessing the splint and dressing. It definitely looked decent. The painkillers had lessened the torture too. 'Thank you, sister.'

Riley nodded and smiled thinly, yet there was no sunny sparkle in those unfathomable caerulean eyes. 'We'll have to go back,' she said, staring down the road to Windermere. The gloom had returned to her.

He tried to move, yelped and fell hard back to the tarmac.

'Hey, easy. You ain't walking and I ain't carrying you, for sure.' She looked at the stile, the lengths of wood.

'No good, all rotten,' said Kayden, tracking her gaze, reading her thoughts. 'My pack. There's a survival knife, para cord and one of those orange survival bags.' Instinct, and his days hanging out with his father had led him to pack them. Riley slipped Kayden's pack off, he winced, grinding his teeth.

He thought of his leg, thought of infection and then of Dorn; how he would be joining him a lot sooner than he had supposed.

Rifling through his pack in a composed manner that pleased Kayden, Riley finally came up with the items. 'What am I doing with these?' Kayden nodded to the birch not far over the other side of the drystone wall.

'Quickly. Cut two thick branches. Use the cord to lash the bag to each of them like a—'

'—stretcher. Nice,' said Riley, with swiftness in her breath and determination in her eyes, she set right to it.

Riley worked fast and seemed pleased with the results. Again, and foolishly so if he admitted, Kayden tried to move himself. He yelled out this time, regretting it that instant. A bolt of lightning struck up his leg, along that side all the way to his head. He writhed like a fish cast ashore. Riley crouched to him, her face a mix of empathic anguish and terror. His yell was answered. The shrieks rose up like some demented bird song.

'We have to go,' he urged, eyes fixed on the way they had come. 'Riley, we have to.'

Another shriek. Louder this time. From which side of the road Kayden couldn't fathom. They would be coming through the trees. No doubt he and Riley would be seeing them soon enough.

'Will it hold?' she asked as she helped Kayden ease up and onto the stretcher.

'We can hope,' he said, flashing a smile that probably told her the pain killers weren't having much effect anymore. She shouldered her pack and lay Kayden's gently in his waiting arms. Dashing round to the head end, Riley took up the two branches as though lifting a wheelbarrow backwards.

'Damn it, Kayden, you're as heavy as hell. End of

the world and you're still a weight. I swear it's that blanket you're wearing.'

'Robes,' Kayden wheezed weakly, fighting back the urge to yelp. Riley huffed and began to heave, ignoring the growing screams in the near distance. Starting off seemed a pain for her but once she got going, she soon got into a decent stride.

'It seems kinda stupid don't it?' she wheezed as she dragged him scraping down the street. 'Going straight to them like this.'

'A little further,' said Kayden, 'there was a—'

'—cottage. I know.'

Riley came to a halt at the place. A quaint grey stone cottage, spore speckled ivy creeping its walls, flowers distorted into some new species. Neither of them had long to admire the impressionist smattering of colour. A shriek rang out to their left a way down the road. There loped a shaded figure, hunched and wild. Behind it more were slipping onto the road from the trees behind the drystone wall like pools of ugly darkness against the beautiful painter's palate of the new world the spore had created.

'Inside' called Kayden. 'Quick!'

Riley's eyes were wide like a despairing philosophical goldfish suddenly dawning it was stuck in a bowl. Kayden could see she wanted to run. To go back to being alone in the woods, just getting by. He saw the battle there, deep in the black wells of her pupils as the light faded from the day. He wouldn't blame her. Watching someone die was bad enough, but seeing someone taken by these monsters...

'Hang on,' she said as she whirled him around in a wild arc leaving splinters of wood and sappy smears ground into the tarmac. Kayden feared he would tumble from his stretcher. Instead of losing him, Riley managed to thread her way through the open gateway and down a narrowing passage.

She kicked in the faded sky-blue door and laboured to bring Kayden into the sanctuary of the kitchen. Riley backed into the dark depths of the house. As she negotiated a doorway, she caught his leg and the agony forced a yell past his lips and that drew the first of those who followed to hinder the light coming through the kitchen door.

Beneath matted tendrils of black hair that masked the humanity of its face was the sharp grin of a hunter that knew it had cornered its prey. Stooped there, its body trembled with the anticipation of a kill, frenzied eyes glinting. Fresh, untainted meat was hard to come by these days. The follower's chest heaved with the ragged breaths of pursuit as it balled its fists, cracking dry skin. It lurched in, another falling immediately in its wake, then another and another.

In his faltering vision, between fits of searing pain and through teary eyes, Kayden saw the sparkle of something hit the first intruder square in the chest. It bounced harmlessly off the thing and came to the floor rolling silver in the light.

A ball of foil.

The room filled with stunning incandescent light, throbbing and pulsating, shimmering like waves. A light of which Riley was the only logical source. An oscillating luminous blue-green glow engulfed the followers in the shaded confines of the kitchen, pouring from her. Kayden's world turned grey and consciousness left him.

Slits of daylight came at first. White light so bright, so piercing. Kayden scrunched his eyes shut again. Waited for the light show to dissipate. He tried again, strained to open his eyes wider this time. It was day, or maybe morning. He couldn't tell either way. His eyes felt like they hadn't been open for years.

'You're awake!' Riley's voice was a noisy excitement mixed with relief. 'Kayden, I thought the spore had taken you.' She laughed and he felt her arms around him, pulling him up from his bed there on the floor in the house. She had seen to his comfort then.

'I don't understand,' he said croakily, throat awkward with speech.

'You have been under for a week. I thought they might have taken you completely after all. But you are okay,' said Riley in a manner he was unaccustomed to. Her accent had softened and her use of English seemed more polished. She passed him some water.

Kayden's mind, still fuzzy, was struggling to make sense of what Riley said and how she had articulated it. A week? Asleep for a week? It all came to him in droplets. The house, the spore, his leg. He sipped the water. It was warm but the moisture was welcome.

Then he realised something—his leg.

There was no pain. He looked down at it and couldn't keep the astonishment from his face. Kayden wiggled his toes and bent his leg at the knee. Nothing, no pain at all. It was healed. He looked at Riley incredulously, that was when he noticed her foil hat was gone. It all came back to him and he looked feverously about the room.

'I took them outside. There's a polyethene tunnel out back, in the garden. They are sheltered,' said Riley in a calm, well pronounced manner. 'They were not harmed.'

'How long have you been with spore?' asked Kayden in a poised tone. He should have been scared; his guard was down. He was in a dark, dry house. They had taken him. He had felt it. Yet he was not frightened, could hear them inside his head almost.

'Since the beginning,' she said finally. *We are not like the others though Kayden,* came a secondary set of voices, echoes in his own mind but coming from her. She crouched slowly, gently. *We promise. We are not like them. They were frightened. When our kind encountered your people, we found such fear, such hate. So, we shut you all down. For your sake and ours.*

'They are living inside us, right now,' Riley said, tapping her head. *We fixed your leg—this mind.* Riley gestured to herself but Kayden knew it was the spore that really moved her limbs.

'Why the deception?' asked Kayden, easing up onto his haunches. 'Why the hat?'

'Persecution Kayden. Those who hide from them, those whose minds are not lost to madness.' She gestured to the outside, to where she had placed the followers.

Most are not ready for such a union. They beat this vessel, cast it out. They would have killed Riley had we not intervened. It seems when faced with a true release from suffering, humans are loathed to let go of that suffering.

'Some say our suffering defines us.'

'So, this is reason to cause it? Kayden, you of all humans should know the difference between solicited and unsolicited suffering. That the former outweighs the later.'

How much pain could be avoided if humans saw that? If you were all linked as we are.

He couldn't argue with that. Frightened people sometimes acted in ways that stripped them of humanity. He had seen it all too often as of late. But was this the only answer?

She was different Kayden. No fear, no hate. We like her as we like you.

'As for the hat,' Riley said aloud, regarding the foil ball which lay as it had fallen, 'it seems humans accept madness over harmony.' Her eyes flicked to his and he witnessed that same glimmer.

Whether it was Riley's glimmer or Riley plus spore, he could not distinguish. Had he ever truly met Riley? *He* certainly felt himself. He regarded his palms, turning them over and over before his eyes.

'You will remain unchanged Kayden,' said Riley

We have strange reactions to the other lifeforms on your planet, we lose a sense of ourselves, become feral, wild. With you humans, the connection is different—more harmonious, except for the fear of course. We merely need a vessel. Shelter from light. This is all.

'At what cost?' he asked looking up to meet her eyes. 'Is it not mind control? I assume you suppressed something in Riley? Suppressed the addict in her, brainwashed her?'

'We simply allow sight Kayden. Allow the human mind to see beyond its limitations. This is therapy enough,' they appealed through her.

'Yes. *Human* limitations. Exactly that,' he said, softly but firmly. The spore had to understand this. 'Take that away or suppress it and what do we have?' He thought on his own words. The implications of a human-spore alliance.

Was is it the natural way of things? Perhaps his thinking was too earth-bound. That these aliens weren't that alien after all. That the extra-terrestrial spore was no different to their terrestrial counterparts. After all, it was all just space dust, right?

He thought hard and silently about it over a lunch Riley prepared. He meditated with his spore mind.

Ate dinner and slept and when Kayden awoke the next morning, feeling refreshed from his first proper sleep in a long time, feeling safe for the first time in a long time, he had made up his mind.

'If this is going to work sister, we need to talk,' said Kayden, eyes fixed on hers, sincerity in his frown. 'To the spore, all of it. Show me everything you have seen, all the worlds you have visited, all the species you have met.'

He had seen glimpses, felt things, they hadn't shown him all yet. Kayden was still uncertain as to what the spore was hiding and why. But he had a responsibility now. He had unwittingly become an ambassador for the human race as had Riley and was still organising that notion in his mind. In his hands he had the destiny of all humans and supposed himself akin to a hesitant god, or a demi-god maybe. After all, the spore had replaced the old gods: commerce and consumerism.

He hadn't asked for such a responsibility, yet here he was. He had been chosen. Either strike a deal or condemn humanity to spore sleep and finally, condemn both species to death leaving the world to the feral mutations. He laughed inwardly at the absurdity of it. All this power yet ultimately both parties were bound by the fear of some kind of extinction. He found himself rolling the same question over and over in his mind; do we truly have a will of our own, or are we all simply feeding the gods?

RECONFIGURED

Drifting. Power drained. Dark. Spinning with the rest of the junk. Hulking carcasses of tattered Nano-composite hull, canisters, undetonated shells. Spewed into cosmos. Remnants of battle. Nearby, an x-ray binary winks its pilot-light blue flame, a neutron star ripping matter from its cohort.

10:01:59

Oxygen readout low. Cabin temperature dropping rapidly. It's already -10°C. Fingers numb, even in these gloves. Our tomb corkscrews along. The inertia of battle blast. We're scuttled, propelled onwards way out of the cargo shipping lanes deep into the void away from war.

I know this fraction of the ship is unhurriedly trying to heal. It groans now and then; the Smart Hull working, absorbing rippling clouds of cosmic dust rolled out on solar winds. Interstellar matter, the building blocks of new worlds. Worlds destined to grow, and if the conditions are just right, spawn life. And perhaps they too will propel themselves to the heavens in metal shells strapped to rockets only to be lost. Like us.

Prisoners of the vacuum. Canned life.

We had no time to don our vacuum suits, only enough to reach a hab-pod. And here we are, a sacrificial offering to the voracious god of intergalactic expansion.

I can almost feel the nano-assemblers reconnecting the wires beneath the ship's skin. Everywhere, alive with them. The hull, the ship's hide, breathing. Reconfiguring.

Minds wander in such cold. I gaze through infrared goggles at the magnificent gamut of colours splashed over the black canvas of space, a spatter of stars, a ghosting of dust.

It touches the soul on a level beyond my clumsy expression of it. I can't bear to gaze any longer. I turn away and rest the goggles on my lap. My mind rests on my breast pocket. It's a pit of darkness in which I don't wish to dwell. Glancing the oxygen readout, I really wish I hadn't. There's no need—I know which way the numbers go.

09:22:05

Systems Tech Nowak is wedged between the bulk head and the oxygen tank, headtorch flickering the last of its light on a crumpled, war-gnawed photo of his two sons, Natan and Konrad, in the arms of their mother, Aurelia.

I remember the photo well.

Nowak had shown me before we shipped. Had been so proud of his family. Aurelia was a beauty. I remember long silken hair framing delicate features, skin pale like bone china. Their boys took after their mother, luckily. Nowak was no looker, but he was a damn fine technician. Must have frustrated him, this helplessness. Trapped in this tin can with minimal systems and no tools.

I imagine myself in that photo, instead of Nowak. The borrowed love warms me, stokes the glowing embers of life within. Nowak's eyes are still lost in Aurelia's unblinking gaze—even now. He told me it was taken at the time he'd promised to return. Promised that the campaign wouldn't steal him like it had her brother. Sweet lies.

Rending sounds fill the interior of the cabin, blast rippled nano-metal straightening, ironing out creases. No one takes notice.

07:32:00

Aft sits Communications Officer Jena—Twenty something. Beneath angular brows, thick and dark, her eyes still carry a burden. I see it in that unfathomable gaze of hers. Green, I think, but in the flickering light of Nowak's head torch they are two black holes. She is sat under a sprawling old oak with her grandmother, I guess. She had spent her last moments there before leaving to fight for a galactic power that would never appreciate her sacrifice.

04:05:48

Above, lying on the roof in the zero-G is Engineer Eirik, a pissed off expression fossilised there in his already gaunt features. Hopeless and pissed off. Most likely annoyed he hadn't been stranded in the mess pod. Definitely pissed off there was no whiskey. Now was the time for drinking. But there is nothing. No food, no drink, no stimulants—not even enough air.

03:17:09

Below Eirik is Lieutenant Yadira in the creeping cold, still grasping the read-out pad, the words: COLLISION IMMINENT, frozen in green electronic hues illuminating the blame and hurt frozen on her face.

And me, Gunner, Private Machiko. In this pod by pure panic-ridden chance. I had simply dashed left instead of right during the evacuation. Had watched the lifeboats power away. I have no parents to speak of, no loved ones to take pictures of and mourn, no addictions or vices unquenched to twist me and no guilt of duties unfulfilled to wrack my last moments. Nothing but the resplendence of my killer; the cosmos and its suffocating kiss.

01:17:09

All is quiet of a sudden. The cabin's hull has healed itself now, reconfigured. The irony is not lost as I stare at the oxygen readout, willing numbers to tick up instead of down. Maybe it has even started to warm up a little. Hard to tell.

My mind is pulled to my breast pocket—the cyanide capsule. Still can't do it. Not like them, not like the others. I'm drawn to the goggles again, peering out through the quartz glass porthole—my soul stolen by a dwarf star. It's like the eye of some long-forgotten god. Its pupil a deep azure of oxygen blue tinged hydrogen green. Its iris, petals of nitrogen red, a flaring disc so vast, so consuming.

00:10:00

In this pod, I will not remain, not in this tomb. I manage to stand, to override the door. There is no airlock, this is no lifeboat. There, on the brink, knowing I have fifteen seconds of consciousness left as soon as I step out into vacuum, I imagine after the drawn out freezing of my body I will drift for millennia, like a comet. Perhaps someday a nearby sun will grant me a magnificent tail of silver-white.

00:00:06

The door slides up. I breath out hard and wish to be a comet, to be spied by some far off civilisation one day.

I wish to be a good omen. To be reconfigured.

A SEA OF SISTERS

Buds blossom beneath the flame-white light of the fire eye, the day forever warmed beneath its liquid glow. The light shimmering through the cracked shells of their hives. Spore erupt from the fleshy flowers of corpses bursting into the stifling air. I see their coldness against it; the colour of spore. Tiny blue-black orbs, their fine tendrils climbing ladders of air. Dancing upward. Such a joyous happening. Living dust on the thermals of the forever-day.

They can't see the spore.

Those who descend from the sky. Those whose shells tear apart with ease like the soft flesh of a youngling.

We catch the scent of their feelings, hear their thoughts—their mostly empty minds—before spore sleep takes them.

Only wilting flowers do they see, those who come after the spawning. Soon will come the new brood, and soon more of *them*. Weak, soft things. They'll descend, burrow and dig. Construct their feeble hives again. Wave, after wave, after wave of them. Like those millennia before. A spreading fungus in need of cleansing.

As the red fire eye crawls high in the creeping day, we watch—us warriors.

We watch. We listen.

Antennae sifting vibrations. Complex eyes perceiving heat.

Always causing such a disturbance, we locate them easily. This kind come engulfed in noise, emitting vibrations, arriving in hard shells not unlike like ours. But our shells are us, not something in which to travel. Our spore, that's how we travel boundless distances, drifting on the warm wind.

They communicate in noise too, loud clumsy sounds. Unsophisticated, blasting din. Even their minds clatter.

We have no need for it. No need for such barbaric resonances.

They are coming, sends sister. She is right. She feels it too.

I know, I deliver my mind to hers, *I hear their thoughts. They are afraid.* My feelings are piercing like light. My mandibles chitter in anticipation of battle.

We must warn the colony. I secrete a marker, a scent signature on the smooth rock. A signal to other clans.

The time has finally come—the drought is over.

The staging area is humming with life. An undulating mass of troopers trekking across the deck with stony faces of resignation. They know, as I do, what's about to go down. Maybe those things down on Zarmina do too. My lieutenant reckons they know. She'd let it slip in the mess hall.

She even believes they think like us.

The colonel disagrees; says they're all vile insects and must be exterminated. Says he's sick of sending troops on missions like this. Sick of mopping up the mess, that this time will be the last. Not because of any sense of paternal duty. Not because of the trauma and loss of life. We're just skins after all. No. He's off schedule, out of time and out of skins.

The *USN Sigma* is almost bereft of troops. We're the last, fresh out the tanks, minds downloaded. Our own deaths fresh in our heads. The last signals our suits sent after the complete balls-up in the southern territories. And for what? A forsaken rock twenty-lightyears from home. An outpost.

But this planet has a strange pull, a mysterious allure that us inquisitive monkeys just can't let go. So, they send in us clones, again and again. Waves after wave. We fight, we die, we fight again. We die too many times, we're wiped. No upload, just a fresh skin

126

born into battle sims and dropped on a rock, to fight and die. Die and fight.

We're certain they'll wipe us after this burn and start fresh in a few years when the next batch is cooked. We've died too many times, the trauma sticks. They say it degrades our performance in the field.

'Casualties?' The colonel seems to be in a dark mood. Grey eyebrows bristling into a frown over distant eyes.

'Two hundred colonists and the entire military escort.' My voice doesn't betray the disgust I feel to be in his presence.

He coughs out a sweet cigar cloud. 'Well, shit.'

I examine the deck below, focusing on the troops and the TOTs, Trans Orbital Transports, they're piling into. They're powering up and filling fast. Heavy Guns, Tech-Mech Armour Clads and KBO, keep bullets out, armour clad troops, support personnel, the Med Corps...

Everyone's invited to the party.

A covert glance to my right and I notice the colonel has joined me on the safety rail now. No longer stiffly standing by but slouched so the height difference isn't so noticeable—us suprehumans are much taller than pure-genes and it narks the colonel.

Surely, he knows it's a death sentence.

The stogie between his fat rubbery lips is sopping wet. Nerves? Maybe. But not about the human loss; the colonists, nor the inevitable troop losses. As he observes the battle group forming below, he knows. Final orders, from the top. No excuses—end it.

And he's coming with us this time, I guess even the brass get punished from time to time. At least they get to hold on to their minds their whole life.

'D'ya know how much that facility cost Captain?' He almost sounds like he's bought the bullshit they're selling him.

I don't reply, nor do I need to. It isn't a question requiring an answer.

'More than you could imagine in your wildest wet dreams, I'd say. Do you even have those?' He snorts at his own joke, but there's no humour in it. No jollity, just grim recognition that the figure is greater than his own worth as a pure born mono-lifer. 'They need to answer for this, you know. They've cost us, those *things*. We have a name for 'em yet son?'

Son he says. Son. I may be an androgyne like all the other troopers, but like most of them, I identify as a female. I swear he does it to piss us off, I want to take him down to the deck, knock the concept into him, but I remain tight lipped and shake my head— negatory.

No biologist has lived long enough to come up with a name.

His pitted raspberry nose twitches in anticipation

of bloodshed. I'm not certain whose exactly.

'Well, probably shouldn't bother.' He shrugs. 'Won't be much of 'em left after the air assault. We'll have our justice.' His barking laughter, wheezing chokes of twisted smoke—they sicken me. Even he doesn't believe his own mendacity. It's as plain as a red-hot Zarminian day. Etched in the canyons of his terrified brow.

His sun scarred face reminds me a lot of Zarmina.

The sunward side; perpetual redness, gnarled outcrops carved out by unrelenting scorching winds. A certain grittiness to it, the faded echoes of lost hope. I see it all, right there, right before me.

Justice?

I snort, he doesn't notice, too wrapped up in his own veiled despair. The word rings ironically in my head. *Justice.* We find ourselves in the constellation of Libra, the scales of justice, yet there seems to be very little justice going around. For us or for those things.

'You hear how it went down son?' The colonel cocks his head; I'm permitted to speak now.

'They're parasitoid extremophiles—'

'What now?'

Let me finish asshole, and I'll tell you.

'Kinda use fungal spores. That's how they've spread so far across Zarmina. On the breeze.'

'They got through the colony's scrubbers? Through their suit filters?' he asks. Now he seems worried.

'No, the scrubbers in the domes worked fine. Nothing passed through the O_2 slaves. Domes one through three were secure...'

'Until they got in.'

'Yeah. Until they got in. After that... It was carnage.'

I watch as infantry, along with the Heavy Guns, filter into their TOTs. A trooper down below guides a gorilla-like Armour Clad into Beta Company's TOT. Huge clomping steps, each one capable of pulping a human into a thick gooey paste.

'Seems their death is just the next phase.' My remark is almost lost in the whining of the Armour Clad's hydraulics.

'Phase?' The colonel rubs his cigar out on the rail. My gaze follows the cascading embers down to the sealed armour of the Tech-Mech, pouring off like sand off a glass ball.

'Certain types sprout some kinda mushroom crap. Dusts up the place with the spores. Anything unmasked gets a dose.'

I've had enough of people-watching and turn around to perch my backside on the rail. Not facing him, but close enough as I can bear. 'Camera footage shows the things ripping suits off colonists. They *peeled* the Armour Clad apart.'

The colonel chokes on thin air. Had he not even bothered to watch the footage himself? Read the reports? Was he that apathetic about the whole matter? This was just a pain-in-the-ass posting to him. Wasn't it? A blip in his career he just wanted over with.

I swallow my smile at his shock and ignorance. 'Soon as the colonists were hit with the spores, they dropped to the deck.'

'I've not seen the vid feed.' He's nervous now, fiddling with his KBO chest plate.

'Probably for the best.' *The troops nearly puked. It'd be too much for you.*

'So—after that?'

He must be nervous to let that remark slip. *Shit. You really want to know?* 'Gestation is rapid, only a couple Earth days. After that, thousands of pupae erupt from beneath the host's skin.' It's painful, really painful. The colonists were alive when it had happened.

The colonel dry swallows and it's clear he's craping his battle fatigues.

'Damn animals. If they were civilised, we'd speak to them.' He turns from the rail patting down the tactical chest rig strapped over his armour. He finds the pouch he's looking for and pulls out another stogie.

'Have we even tried?' I ask.

He barks out a sardonic laugh and spits. 'Talk? To those *creatures*? How?'

A lighter materialises from somewhere, an old brass Zippo, probably antique. His face is horrifying in its glow. Like some god caught in the glow of a burning world it has just laid waste to.

'And why?' he asks, simultaneously drawing on the stogie. He puffs a bluish cloud of smoke into the tense air. He snorts. 'They can't be intelligent. They're just animals.'

Silence as he rests in his arrogant self-assuredness.

What makes you so sure? Just because they don't speak like us, don't build like us. Is that the measure of intelligence? Of civilisation? I'm not so sure. Nothing is certain for me anymore.

'Careful.' The colonel is looking straight at me now, narrow eyes accusing me of something.

I search my facial muscles. Had I lost it for a minute? Had my composure evaporated and he'd seen the doubt beneath? Read my mind?

'Don't think I haven't seen that look before *son*.' The last word is meant to hurt. I can see it in his penetrating stare as he points at me with his smouldering cigar—dressing me down.

'You're a soldier. *We* made you, augmented you, sculpted you. You don't have a mommy or daddy.

You're battle built, just like the Armour Clads and the Heavy Guns down there—weapons. You belong to us and don't you forget it. That's the trouble with you Initials. Think your human...'

I see it in his eyes, what he's thinking, to make a note on my file for the techs back in the labs; dump memory, not for regeneration.

As if in answer to my mental pleas for the moment to be over, the *Sigma's* deck sirens blare and it's to the TOTs, strapped in and birthed out of the *Sigma* into Zarmina's atmosphere before we know it.

The burn in is rough—it's always rough.

The dull red glow of Gliese 581 bathes the TOT's interior in lava light. Faces within Tactical Breather Helmets, they're glad for the masks, the troops. I know they are. Can't see dread through mirrored visors. Everyone's thinking it, this could be our last chance; survive or get wiped into oblivion. Dying for real.

Right now, my suit's talking to the *Sigma*. It says it's a blistering day on Zarmina. On the sunny side of the silicate rock giant at least, a roasting 90°C. But on the dark side of the tidally locked planet—nothing but ice. Why the hell couldn't the drill teams have just stayed there? Why'd they have to poke around and taunt the demon?

As we leave the huge razor slice of smooth stone we call cresting rock, more blasts rattle us from above.

Heat and noise bathe our dull triangular carapaces and ribbed abdomens. Dusting us in desert reds and ochres. Their flying shells, their angular egg pods. Whatever they are—strange ways they travel. The soft ones have come for revenge. For what we did to their hive.

It's going to be bad this time. Sister stinks of fear.

She can be forgiven, it's not a weakness. Her concern for her sisters and our mother overwhelms me with adoration for her.

When they dug into the southern clan's nest and took the young, my thoughts are tainted with compassion, *when they tore them to pieces… That was bad. This will be justice.*

I sense her doubt. *But sister, could we have not hidden beneath them?*

I pity her. She can feel it I'm sure. *For thousands of cycles we have lain dormant. This is our way—our cycle. What do you fear sister?*

She does not answer. Her thoughts are muddled.

How did you feel ten cycles ago? The question is a simple one, I feel the stirrings of an answer, the logical truth. The only answer she can give.

Nothing. I felt nothing.

And why was that? She knows I'm leading her; she can feel it. Nothing is hidden between us, between any of us.

I had not been hatched sister. Neither of us had.

And what will you feel after the spawning? I send.

The point is made, I know it. *Nothing. I will be dead.*

Then what is there to fear now? I send her love, compassion. *It is the way of life. We are born to die sister. And when we die, we create.*

We share a moment, antennae interlocked. At one, at peace. We think in unison. *There is balance.*

Soon we are skittering over rock, wading through sand drifts and disappearing into our burrow. Its warmth engulfs us, swallows us. Here it is moist, damp. Humidity saturates our shells, allowing us to grow.

Up there, we are as hard as the smooth ridge I marked. And as sharp. My forelegs are slicers, my mid-legs hold back even the strongest and my rear kickers decapitate.

We scurry along twisting tunnels past loyal workers, their minds looped in devoted regularity. Dig, clean, carry. Dig, clean, carry. It's all they can think, want to think.

To serve their colony, their sisters, their mother.

We all want nothing else; we live for her. For the good of the colony.

Sister's thoughts feel like my own. Loud in my head. *There's more this time. More flying shells. That means many soft ones inside.* Sister paused, mandibles clacketing loudly. A sign of fear returning.

Your concerns are unfounded sister. This is simply our cycle, no matter how the in-between occurs, we come to the same end. I release yet more calming pheromones.

Her antennae twitch and sweep. We touch, connected. More gather around us in the tunnel, drawn by our mind waves and scent. *Follow.* That's the feeling. *Follow.*

There we stand, motionless. It would be silent but for our chittering mandibles. Sisters, connected we start toward her, towards our wonderful mother.

Buzzing. All around. Alarms are droning now. The TOT's thrusters are compensating and the pilot's doing a grand job of shaking us up like a can of cheap beer. A jolt and a battering cacophony and I know we're about to hit dirt.

I hear a squawk over the comms. We all do. Something's up with the pilot, she's not making any sense. Another jolt. Wind shears? No, not wind shears.

A searing pain in my head, a fleeting fuzziness.

Another radio squawk and this time a scream. The troops cringe, desperately clawing at the side their helmets attempting to turn down their receivers.

The TOT lunges downward and the troops of Alpha Company are breathing out their fair share of gut plunging moans. It's pretty obvious we are in free fall.

'We're gonna die,' says someone, who, it doesn't matter.

'Then you re-skin. So what? Screw it down private.' My bark is so loud and firm I almost convince myself, but something tells me we won't be uploading after this burn.

No one makes another sound after that. They're all trying to relax their bodies, like me, to minimize injury when we imp—

We hit hard, grinding into the planet.

A summersault. Shouts, screeching and rending metal. A snapping of something that shouldn't snap. More shouts, a yelp of pain.

'Ride it out! Ride it out!' I shout, hoping someone is alive to hear it.

Black. Steam. Searing joints.

I'm okay, I'm okay. Okay, okay. All's good. Get up. Get up. Get up!

I'm crawling on my belly like a reptile.

Goddamit.

There's a crack in my visor and for some reason I can't see out clearly, my suit is pretty pissed— screaming its alarm. I reach around.

'Shit!'

My chest rig has gone. Panic begins to set in, if I

repeat my failure in the south, if I die, they'll dump my memory for certain this time and start afresh. I feel faint, my stomach churns and there's some mystery pain in my lower back.

Breathe. Breathe damn you! Breathe. Suck it in.

I breathe.

A deep belly breath—as much as my restrictive armour allows. Now I'm focused on the ground. Around me; twisted remains of Heavy Guns, like giant spiders, dead on their backs.

Damn.

No rail guns. I snap at myself. Shouting at my own wandering mind. *Focus!*

I see it then, my chest rig, somehow tangled up in the mechanical feet of an Armour Clad. It's funny how mind-twisting things happen in a crash, how you can end up almost undressed by a two tonne Mech suit and still be alive. It's not moving, so I assume the pilot is either unconscious or dead.

I'm heaving myself along now, stretching the pain out of my muscles. Good. I'm okay, everything's probably still attached and where it should be. That's when I notice the smell. The bitter stench of puke. Had I been sick? Possible, it *was* a rough landing.

A thought occurs to me and I pause to lean and access my helmet vent. I hold my breath and press it. The visor clears, the vomit sucked out by the helmet's tech. Nice touch, I'll thank the tech crews who thought of the feature later—if I make it.

Funny. Maybe there's hope for the mission yet.

Another moment and I've flooded my helmet with oxygen again, but I'm still losing some through the crack, not enough to die soon, but enough to concern my suit. I need my rig.

It's an arduous crawl but I finally get to the Armour Clad and snag my rig from its foot. It's too light, and yet again I marvel at how a spinning ship can empty an emergency pouch so efficiently and leave no trace strewn anywhere.

'Great.' My voice booms in my own ears.

'Captain?'

It takes me a moment, but I recognise my Lieutenant's voice.

'Captain? Is that you?' Her voice fizzes and pops over the comms, but she sounds good. No trace of injury in her voice.

'Yeah.' I manage a drawn reply, full of pain. 'Where are you?'

'Outside sir.'

'What! How the hell?'

'Dunno sir, just came to out here. Your guess is as good as mine.'

'Report.' I'm straight to business, but still trying to

visually locate my emergency patch kit.

'It's FUBAR sir.'

'That bad?' I'm gasping now. 'Look, I need a patch kit. I'm in the troop bay, next to an Armour Clad. Do me a solid, would you?'

She is with me in a moment, her boots a welcome sight. She crouches and sees to my visor first, using her kit. She is silent the whole time, shock no doubt. Taking my gloved hand, she heaves me to my feet and guides me out of the wrecked TOT.

'You okay sir?'

I dust myself off. 'Fine. Still here.' I imagine her smiling, but her face is a silver blank. My KBO armour boots crunch into the red shale surface and I survey the area.

We're just off the Gliese Geological Survey from what I can see, so we made the landing area—sort of. The Vogt colony's three geodesic domes are nothing but shattered dust-filled shells behind us. They look like huge eggs, fractured and drained of life.

The would-be staging area is a mess. Downed TOTs and mangled gear. I hear a roar over our heads and watch as the colonel's TOT drops down safely unscathed amidst the cover of the decimated colony. Typical.

'Sir.' My lieutenant surprises me a little, I'd forgotten there were other survivors for a moment, lost in the darkness that had consumed the mission. I don't let on.

'Report.' All business. No emotion. Just a cool calm killer. Right, like I believe that. I still try to lie to myself. They say for a convincing lie you first have to convince yourself. If I believe it, the brass believes it. It doesn't show on the uploads and you pass into the next skin, the same mind, safe.

'Information's trickling in sir, but this is what we've got… Heavy Guns from Alpha and Beta companies are gone, their ACs too. Beta took huge loses sir. Something messing with the pilot's head during the drop. Equipment malfunction maybe.'

Something doesn't sit right with me there, I let it slip for the moment.

'What about the others?'

'Gamma company made it down okay and are setting up a perimeter. Delta and Zeta have dropped on Vogt's perimeter under the colonel's orders. They were the last down so had a little warning sir. Pilots managed to wrangle the ships in safely. Omega company has located itself in a central command position within the colony. Sir.'

There's something else, a pregnant pause.

'Sir…'

'Lieutenant. A problem?'

She hangs her head, the motion just barely visible in her bulky KBO suit. 'It's Epsilon company sir…'

I look around the landing field, the steaming piles of junk and wrecked transports. My guts sink, heavy and hot like molten metal.

'Shit. Where are they?'

'It happened as soon as they landed sir. The surface it—it just gave way. The whole TOT fell into the pit sir.'

I straighten up, harden my voice, swallowing the catch in my throat. 'Survivors?'

'Negative. The fuel cell struck; the blast nearly took out Beta group as they were climbing out of their TOT according to their CO.'

'We're running low on troopers.' My disappointment goes unchecked. It's a numbers game and we were losing. We both know we aren't just fighting this battle, but also fighting for our minds. The stakes were high now, and everybody knows it.

'Afraid so sir. We've got the surviving ACs patrolling the perimeter.'

'Any sign of the locals?' I ask as I cross my eyes trying to examine the sealed crack in my visor. It's going to be a pain in the ass, cutting through my line of sight like that.

'No sir. No attack, nothing.'

'No attack?' I laugh, louder than I should. I gesture the wreckage with a sweeping arm. 'What the hell do you think that was? A welcoming dance?'

'You think *they* caused all this?' She sounds almost incredulous, but something in her voice tells me she's not totally opposed to the concept.

I watch as troopers drag weapons from the wreckage, sorting themselves out, salvaging what they can. 'You don't?'

She answers after a few moments of silence. 'Now that you mention it, I felt a little fuzzy on the way down. Thought it was just nerves.'

'Yeah, me too. Didn't give it a thought.'

'But how?' She unconsciously takes her weapon through a function check. Her actions are effortless and smooth. Clockwork. It's a good idea, so I follow suit.

'We don't know anything about them.' I pop the cartridge out and run through safe, semi and burst— the hammer falling when it's supposed to. Content the action is clean, I slam the cartridge back in and give my rifle the once over. It looks a little bashed up, but functional.

'What we *do* know is the colony wasn't breached.' I wait for the shocked reaction I know is coming.

'What? But I thought—'

'Yeah, well. They kept it hush for a reason.' There was no point in keeping secrets now, so I spill the beans. It feels good to be open. I always hated keeping secrets from my troopers. 'The colonists opened the doors.'

'They what!'

I shake my head, regret for not having seen it for what it was. 'We didn't put two and two together.' I look at the mess we're in—the salvaged Heavy Guns hobbling around like bugs on crutches. 'And we paid for it.'

'Sir...'

There's a quiver in my lieutenant's voice, even over the comms. It's plain fear. She's well aware of the odds. Aware our next upload to the *Sigma* will be dumped or if we're really unlucky, only edited; a fragmented mind was worse than being returned to factory settings as we refer to it. Through good behaviour and stellar performance, I'd managed to hang on to my Initial's mind.

'Something you wanna say lieutenant?' I can sense the question hanging in the shimmering air.

'Sir?' She's hesitant.

'Spit it out lieutenant.' *And hurry, it's probably going to be the last time we speak, in this skin—ever.*

'Are we gonna make it sir? I mean—'

I want to say yes, but I've never been much for sugar-coating things. 'You know the answer lieutenant; descend into death, rise into glory.' She nods. She's well aware of the corps' motto; it's branded across her shoulders after all, along with her service number and skin issue code.

I join her in her gaze over the undulating red desert, beyond a fin shaped ridge that's slicing up out of the ground like a hand held palm up; no trespassing beyond this point.

'Thought this was supposed to be our next best hope,' she says. 'A new home.'

I laugh, louder than perhaps appropriate. 'Yeah well... Probes only show you so much.' I gesture to the open shale desert, the queer bubbling outcrops of igneous rock. 'This is what hope gets you. A kick in the teeth.'

I think about the camera feed again. The tearing skin, the screams. The metamorphosis of pupae into the nymphs, eventually scuttling away.

All because of hope.

'We're like them you know.' Her words are swords. Tempered blades of truth.

'Yeah?' That's all I can manage.

'A disease. A scourge.'

'This *is* their planet,' I respond swiftly. 'But maybe you're right about us. We *are* a disease here. An invasive species. I guess it's all perspective, huh?'

For a second, I question whether I'm talking about us as invading human forces or as skins rather than pure-genes. Either way, I'm not sure if I'm a hundred percent comfortable with the concept of being an invader. Protector, yes. Invader, well, the word has a bitter taste to it. We don't speak for a few minutes, but eventually, it's me who breaks the silence. I turn to her. We can't see each other's expressions but we know. *We know.*

'Regret being cooked up lieutenant?'

She stiffens. 'No sir. It's just—I wonder—'

'If it was them?' I offer. 'The hole, right? Losing Epsilon group. That's what you were thinking.'

'Yeah.' She sighs, a thoughtful pause. 'That would prove it, wouldn't it?'

I look out over a landscape tempered by a molten sun. 'That they are intelligent? Perhaps, or maybe it's just instinct.'

'Like travelling through the galaxy, taking worlds and destroying anything that harms, infects or attacks us? Is that instinct?' The stinging guilt in her voice is plain now.

Guilt. Something they hadn't planned us ever being capable of. Another reason to be defragged. That's what the techs call it. We call it soul death.

'It does make you wonder, doesn't it?'

I won't berate her, not like the colonel did me. She sees it like it is and the time has passed for protocol. Frankness is the order of the hour now.

That's the problem when they create us. They can engineer strength and reflexes but they just can't nail blind faith and unquestioning obedience. Yeah, they try to brainwash us, a tweak here, an edit there, but it doesn't always take. You learn to hide it. Bury it deep; anything to ensure your next upload is unedited. Anything to cling onto yourself.

'What we do today,' she continues, 'the outcome will ignite a chain of events which could damn us as a species.' Her words are the solemn truth as far as she was concerned.

"Us as a species." She regards herself as human. I smile inside. That's something they can't take from us either, no matter how much they tell us we're not, we will always be human.

The colonel, and others like him, would disagree.

The chamber is vast, wall to wall life. Sister workers, an insulating living hollow. Thick, moist air caresses us all as we join the pool of life. Central, in all her swollen grandeur, is mother.

They are coming then. Her soothing signals placate me, a complicated fluttering of her many limbs. Of course, she already knows. *Their intention is extermination. They wish to wipe us clean my child. Burn us out.*

I lower my bristled thorax to the moist soil, spreading my slicers forward, vibrating my abdomen. The dank air whistles though the spines and hollows there. A reverent chirrup. And only on such occasions do we use it—before our beloved mother.

I feel her love in response. We all feel her love. The chamber chitters excitedly, even the workers feel it.

War is coming today mother, I send. She senses the concern hidden within me, something I keep well from the others. But not from her, not from mother.

Look around you child. Her thoughts are pure, soothing pleasure. *Count our numbers, and note how strong we are. Our numbers are vast, like our spore... our kind will persist.*

But mother... Imploring thoughts. For I have seen the skies darken with the swarm, more than ever in our long history. Perhaps sister's fear infecting me. *They are different to those that came before the drought.*

Yes, my child. There are many. They come in their multitudes. We, the mothers of all the clans have focused our minds. We have insured the invaders will lose, of their failure, there is no doubt. She is pleased.

They land south of the crest. Mother, they know you are here.

Yes. Their intention is all but the clearer and your task, my child, is also clear. She never shows fear. Never. We adore her even more for it. *The young have hatched, have they not?*

Yes mother. The bodies of the last brood have served their purpose. I exude pride. The cycle has begun again at long last.

Good. Feelings of joy, satisfaction, contentment. *Then those that come from the sky will truly know their purpose here. There will be balance.*

I gaze upon her with compound eyes, she is a blue flame in the red heat of the royal chamber. Magnificent and terrible.

The colonies have united then? My question is respectfully conveyed.

Yes. Sincerity. Assuredness. *All the colonies, all over the hot side. They have awoken, we have coordinated our summoning powers to lure the hosts. The pull stretches much farther than ever before. The drought of vessels is coming to an end my child. More will come after these vessels are spent. Balance will be restored.*

The second wave of soldiers are already matured. Mother judders, her antennae fluttering. *Whether you survive battle or not, you will have a great honour my precious child. Your consciousness will live on in your children. Each will be you as you are me.* Her antennae twitch and sweep in hypnotic arcs.

She beckons me.

I skitter towards her. She embraces me with gigantic slicers; a gentle mother's embrace. I rear up and our mandibles lock.

The royal jelly is yours my dear. Go fight, cleave the soft ones, separate them from their shells. Soon, you shall bear the buds of age, and when they blossom: queens. Queens my sweet, precious, child. You will further our kind across the land and with them, eons of knowledge. Our legacy.

I allow the thick gelatinous substance to slide

down my throat. Sweet and instantly gratifying. I feel it ebb as it is absorbed into my very being. I know it. I feel it. My carapace flushing iridescently like mother, for I carry the knowledge. I carry my consciousness and now the gift to pass it on. A gift only a few are blessed to receive.

I slope away, workers parting as if I am royalty itself. I am swarmed by sister soldiers, my guard.

Go. Our mother's mind vibrations stir the colony. *Go and sweep the land. You are a devastating sea. Flood the lands, show the soft ones what they really are.*

Her thoughts are power itself. Pure and crystal. We turn and leave the chamber. Millions of us churning to the surface.

A sea of sisters.

Gazing over the ridge, resting in the silence of absent words, my lieutenant and I are lost in the dreams of a far-off planet, a once blue planet. Absentmindedly, we both doublecheck our bayonet broad-blades are fixed securely to our rifles.

I decide the silence is too much like agony, that it's time for some more shop talk to break the mood.

'See that knife ridge?'

'Yes-sir.'

'The CPU on the *Sigma* reckons the nest is over there. Underground.'

'That's why we didn't spot it before sir? Before they built the colony—I mean.'

'No. No, the GGS surveyed the entire area to avoid such situations. They thought the planet was a sterile rock. No homegrown life in the south or here.' Something makes me prime my rifle. 'No, they just seemed to pop up out of nowhere. Who knows, eh?'

'We don't really understand what we're up against, do we sir?' I appreciate her bluntness. The fear has departed.

Good. Better to die resolute than full of fear. She's primed her rifle too. Not in response to me, but intuition. Something we both sense. Off in the distance I eventually spot them. A chitinous mass—the swarm.

'And here they come,' I say. 'Send word to the Colonel, we're due company.'

My lieutenant is fixed for a moment; visualising the battle perhaps. I hope she's imagining the outcome better than I am.

'What are you waiting for? A written request?' I sound like that old hard-ass again. 'War's coming, move it lieutenant!'

Two fronts meet. Metal bugs—Heavy Guns—a tide of carapaced warriors breaking against them. They remind me of when I was a kid, my original self I mean, the first grown, before they developed the tech to pop us out fully grown. I am one of the few who'd played their cards right, kept my Initial's memories.

It was one particularly hot summer and this one day had been deemed too hot for training, so, in an unusually generous gesture, the brass allowed us a few water guns to play with.

It was strange for any of us to have actual free time away from the assault courses and battle conditioning sessions. Probably the only time we were ever truly kids. Now, they just keep the new ones in the tanks. We're all trained through simulations and popped out fully baked. Or in my case, and others like me, rested and regenerated.

Whilst playing seek and destroy with the other cadets, I ran behind the huge green bunkhouse to find a good hiding place and I happened across a huge locust writhing on the path.

I thought it was injured and crouched to help it, maybe give it some food: grass or something. But then, to my shock, I realised it was moving erratically, not because it was injured but because of the ants, thousands of them. Slowly tugging it along. And as if that didn't disturb me enough, bigger ants were shearing off its limbs passing them to the workers. They dismantled it, piece by piece.

I had been so lost in the morbidity of it I hadn't noticed the colonel behind me, only, he wasn't a colonel then. I've never forgotten what he said to me that day.

'See those big ones there, son. You see them?

Soldiers son. Soldiers. That's you and don't you forget it. You take that pity, take it and screw it up into a fist to crush your enemy. Be the soldier ant son. Not the locust.'

That carnage, that was my first experience of death and the true beginning of my life.

What I see now, is no different. Except it isn't locusts being dismantled, it is the Heavy Guns. Metal legs cleaved off. We are the locusts.

The armour clads do no better at holding them back, we are too few and they are vast in their numbers. We can't compete in our fractured state. The tide is fast approaching me and I'm separated from my Lieutenant. Lost in a living black sea.

Their glutinous black blood smears across my cracked silver visor. My rifle's hot. Hotter than it should be. Alpha Company are already a collection of assorted limbs scattered across this cursed dirt, my lieutenant too. I'm pretty sure that I heard her scream over the comms. Not words, but a plea all the same, to bring her back, complete in body and soul. Bring us all back. The CPU back on the *Sigma* must have its work cut out for it. I look up, all those signals, all those souls, flying up right now, uploading.

The whole thing's a mess.

The Armour Clads hold out longest, I think a couple got away too. They'll make it to the colony but not long before the swarm. Too late to secure the Colonel, he'll be minced I bet. Won't be coming back either. Can't say it cuts me up. There's nothing the

Sigma can do either. Napalm didn't work in the south; it won't work here.

I drop my rifle. What's the point? It's all insane, all this death. And for what? I close my eyes and drop to my knees and cry, unable to wipe the tears away, they just roll. Crying is something I've ached to do for such a long time, but was unable to do. They'll reset me for that, I'm certain.

The odd feeling pulses within my chest at first, a warm powerful heaving.

I cry for my lieutenant.

At the end of everything I finally let go. I let go of the hate for the corps, for creating me, for every time they brought us back, for every edited soul, for leaving in the torture and the pain... for bringing me here.

I cry for the dead, the wiped minds, the lost souls.

I let go of the self-loathing I've held onto for all these years, for not rebelling, for not having the courage to say no. For accepting the weak excuse that I was born this way, born a killer.

I cry for that locust.

My eyes are closed so tight, my head hurts. I feel as if I will drown on my own tears if I don't stop but I can't. A bright crystal light floods my vison and for a moment something wild opens up within me.

I hear them—the creatures. The feeling slices

through me like a crystal shard. We have been judged for our greed and wanton destruction of everything we have encountered in our galaxy. Justice is being served.

The sudden horror of all we've done engulfs me and I feel as if I've shed my suit and stepped out into the blazing heat of Zarmina. I let go of my mind, let go of my concept of self and I'm in free fall, connected to everything. Is this their doing? This sight? This vision?

Opening my eyes, I see the battle field with their eyes and as the creatures pass me by, I can hear their devotion, no hate, no malice. They are just doing what they do. Their cycle. Striking a balance.

They pass me by.

Why? Why won't they kill me?

I promise myself, that if I survive, I'll take a TOT and leave. Not return to the *Sigma*, but to the stars. Grow this soul. I'm tired of being reborn, of living forever in this torturous existence. One of the creatures pauses right in front of me and I wonder if it weren't for my suit, would I feel its breath? I close my eyes, only one thought pulsing through my mind. *Forgive us.*

Arriving behind the first wave, already the soft ones litter the dirt, mostly gestating. Limp four limbed flesh sacks. Their odd hairy heads and two eyes. Mouths sporting no mandibles but ugly red fleshy muscle. Others still have fight, those with shells protecting their soft, crunchable heads. Tri-legged walkers lie on the backs, legs torn from them.

They are monsters, there is no doubt in my mind. I hear their thoughts as they lie dying, they think only of themselves. They have a planet of their own, yet they have left it, greedy for more.

No matter.

The sisters showed them the same lack of mercy they showed when they took young ones in the south soon after their arrival, pulling their legs off one at a time.

I smell their fear and feel the frenzy well up within me.

I rear up on my kickers, surveying the desolation. Many sisters have fallen, but more invaders are now with spore. For eons, we have spread in such a manor. Lying dormant, only our mothers conscious in the half-sleep, sending out the call.

Luring potential hosts.

Reinforcements will come, no doubt. Perhaps from the unseen sky hive. But it will be only to gestate the next brood. Some of the sisters are already in their chrysalis stages, and myself too, I can feel the change within me. Soon we will all bear buds on our backs, then the skies will be full of even more spore and I will bear thousands of queens. Only a few will survive to maturity, but that is just the way of things.

As I survey their future kingdom, I see one of the soft ones alive. It seems to be prostrating, lowered in respect perhaps. I approach it, the energy of the killing blow already building up inside me.

As I come in for the strike, I can't help but stop. Something in my head, something alien to me. The creature? Are they intelligent enough to speak with the mind? The concept seems absurd as I stare into its blank silver gaze.

Warmth, sorrow. Mixed together, a jumbled nymph's way of thinking, but the feel of its thought pattern is unmistakable: regret and compassion. I back away slightly and it seems confused. Maybe expects me to kill it.

It stands, feeble and weak from battle. For a moment, it just stares at me. No longer mind-speaking, the moment has gone, the skill has slipped from its beginner's grasp. A pity. We stand together for a few more moments until it gets the idea, I'm letting it go. This one is different. Its genes should not be culled like the rest of them. It is mother's wisdom, so it is mine.

Balance.

As it slowly limps away, I wonder if they love their queen, their colony, in the same way we do. I find it hard to imagine any other way. A blast of emotion hits me again, its mind grasping back the skill one last time perhaps. I sense it won't be coming back, but others will, and they too will die and be reborn.

EDIK THE AUTOTELIC

'My God, Mr. Bartkowski!' said Doctor Wen as Edik entered her office. It was then Edik realised he'd lost so much weight. Once he'd clicked the door shut behind him Doctor Wen had him up on the examination table with his mouth open, tongue depressed and a penlight shoved in there.

She examined him thoroughly and, when finished, removed her blue latex gloves flinging them in a peddle bin beneath a corner sink so clean that it looked freshly installed that morning.

After scrubbing her hands, she seated herself behind an organised desk casually knitting her fingers on her lap in her usual I'm listening posture. The smile she flashed lifted Edik's mood a little.

'Tell me Mr. Bartkowski,' she began, her slight Chinese accent creeping through, 'how long have you been this way?'

Edik told her everything, speaking as though some floodgate had opened. He told her that he wasn't sure when he'd started to lose weight or when the insomnia had developed or even the last time he'd eaten, yet he vaguely remembered drinking something and that it had most likely been a strong coffee, though he couldn't be certain and that...

When he finally took a breath, he concluded that what he did know was that his concentrative ability had skyrocketed as if he'd been struck by some muse. He'd finished his book in a matter of days and redrafted it twice. And the other ideas... He'd filled five spiral bound notebooks with bestsellers, he just knew it.

Doctor Wen listened, a patient smile fixed upon her delicate face, dark eyes like black holes drawing in anything that dared venture too close. When Edik finished, she stood and told him she required a stool and urine sample.

When he asked why she explained she'd ruled out depression given how he'd excitedly described his thirst for writing. Bipolar perhaps, on account of his manic state but she was reluctant to label at this stage and was convinced all would come to light with a more thorough examination. She sent him to a nurse telling him the practice would call when the results came through.

As Edik set to producing his samples his mind naturally drifted to the main tenet of his next book.

He shook his head in disbelief. *What am I* doing*? Some terrible muscle wasting disease could be slowly killing me and I'm worried about* my book*?*

But you need *to write.* The voice was so close Edik jumped. He looked around the tiny bathroom then at the urine sample on the shelf. He was still working on the other one.

Forget this, you're fine. Go home.

Edik was glad he was sitting down but not so happy about being trapped in a cubical with a disembodied voice. Was it in his head perhaps? Perhaps it was his muse, every writer had a muse, right?

'Muse?' he said aloud, his voice hollow and trembling echoed in the tiny bathroom.

Yes.

Edik gulped. It was a dry, awkward swallowing of fear and he felt the blood draining to his toes. He grasped the handrails either side of the toilet in case he fainted.

'You're real?'

Yes. There's no need to speak with your mouth. Think and we'll hear you all the same, said the voice.

Edik wasn't sure what frightened him most; that he was talking to his mind and it was responding or that his mind had just referred to itself as *we.*

We are not mind, Edik. We are Muse—if that name

pleases you. He wasn't so sure about being pleased as such, but unnerved, that was for certain.

What do you want? he asked, terrified what another response would say about his mental health.

You write. It feels good, doesn't it? They were right, it *did* feel great.

Now? I have business to do, he thought, looking at the expectant plastic cup next to a urine sample that looked more like a shot of orange juice. *I also need to hydrate.*

No need to finish your business. You can hydrate at home, whilst you write, said the voice that sounded like it had been overlaid upon itself a billion times.

But I have to, he thought, yet could feel his legs tensing to stand even though he hadn't commanded his body to do so.

No, write, said the voices accompanied by an overwhelming urge to stand. Edik felt like a helpless marionette.

For ten minutes he battled the voices. They wanted him to leave, yet he so desperately wanted to finish his sample. In the end, Edik won out, but it was as though his body was in revolt and the only offering he could give to the nurse was miniscule. She said a small sample would be enough.

Embarrassed, Edik left the surgery in a hurry to the niggling chorus in his head; *Write. Write. Write...*

Edik glanced the time in the bottom right of the screen: 06:07. Edik was certain 22:19 had only been a few furiously typed minutes ago. He wrote some more then glanced the time again: 08:02.

What? How is that possible?

Edik scrolled up and down the screen. *No, it can't be... How many words? No. Almost forty thousand?*

Edik fell back in his chair, straightening the night's aches from a back bent crooked from typing. The bright morning blazed in through the window beyond which the waking world buzzed in its brightness. People on the way to work, deliveries being taken, refuse being collected, kids with sullen faces lugging their bags to school.

'But how?' The words lingered on his lips with no one to hear them, except Muse.

We help you. You help us.

He tried to shake the voices from his head, rub the tiredness from his eyes. His eyes...

They stung and no amount of rubbing or drowning with eyedrops could alleviate the soreness. Pushing himself back from the wooden pasting table which served as his writing desk, he stood from the formed plastic chair which seemed more suited to a greasy spoon cafe than a Cambridge flat.

On shaky legs Edik made his way from the pasting

table which served as a desk to the bathroom a few unsteady steps away and grasped aimlessly for the pullcord only to snag it by chance. The light flickered on in the cubed cell which passed for a bathroom and his own pitted eyes snared him in the mirror.

He certainly didn't see himself as the languid, red eyed wraith that stared back from the finger smeared glass. *Reflections rarely lie*, he thought as he scratched the thick carpet of stubble growing on skin stretched too thinly over bone.

Doesn't matter. Just write, said Muse.

He leaned into the mirror out of morbid curiosity, like a rubber-necked motorist drawn to a car crash and with long spidery digits more like twigs than fingers, he pulled down his lower eyelids exposing red flesh.

Blood vessels in fine wormy threads conspired against the dirty yellow mass of his eyeballs. He snapped back in repulsion like a repentant rubbernecker having seen too much.

The toilet beckoned him through remembered habit rather than need. His bladder felt shrivelled and his bowels shrunken against his spine and pelvis as if retreating from some blazing inferno.

There, underpants around ankles, complacence upon his face, he stared at the spiderweb cracks in the ceiling. The cracks he'd told himself he'd fill and paint as soon as he'd papered the front room. He'd got as far as setting up the paste table. That had been last month.

*

Edik tapped end call and sighed, his arm falling limp at his side, hand just barely clutching his phone. The surgery had his results. Yet for some reason he felt no relief.

Muse told him not to bother, that it wasn't important. What was important was to start on his next project.

Pushing back the keypad like an empty plate he sighed again, this time a little longer. It was all happening so fast. He'd sent his manuscript off the day he'd returned from his examination. It had only been a couple of days when an agent called, actually called, and told him with an enthusiasm that staggered him they should meet for coffee right away.

Muse seemed okay with that little trip as it promised more projects in the months and years to come. Ellie, his agent to be, was aghast at his skeletal condition when they first met and hid it poorly. Edik explained it away as a medical condition and after that she had seemed more relaxed.

They got on well. Ellie told him his writing style was like nothing she'd read before, though Edik imagined she was just being kind.

He still had a lot of work to do and Ellie advised him to get started on the second book. He hadn't told her that the whole process had only taken him a few days and that a second was underway. Who would believe that? Did it matter? Muse thought not and seemed pleased with his silence.

As he glanced over at his laptop glowing on his desk, a multi-layered voice called softly to him, *Write*.

Edik lunged into his bedroom with an exaggerated gait like a mime struggling against a robust wind that didn't exist. He tussled with his own body and fought to wrestle his clothes on with his left hand that still had allegiance for him whilst his right, under the control of Muse, tried to tear them back off.

He shambled all the way to the surgery in fits and starts. Five spasming steps forward two back. Passers-by gave him as wide a birth as the pavement would allow and anxious parents guided inquisitive children away from 'the funny man'.

Edik couldn't knock on Doctor Wen's door for the want of trying, so he burst in like a marauding raider and threw himself in the chair muttering about how uncomfortable he felt. Doctor Wen nodded calmly.

'When was the last time you moved your bowels Mr. Bartkowski?' she asked, settling back into her seat after his startling entrance.

He shrugged.

'No wonder you're uncomfortable,' she said.

He didn't think not pooping much would make him this uncomfortable or hear voices. He remained silent though, eager to hear the news.

'You have a bacterial infection of the likes no one has ever seen Mr. Bartkowski.'

No kidding, he thought, but kept his silence allowing her to continue.

'A sample has been sent off to King's College for further study believe it or not. For now, we'll start you off on a course of antibiotics,' she reached for a slip of paper and began to scrawl, 'take this to the pharmacy and follow the dosage instructions—to the letter.' She emphasised the last part, holding his gaze for a moment.

She then sat straight and slid the slip across the desk to him. Edik stared at it for longer than intended and upon realising Doctor Wen's confusion attempted to take the slip but his right arm paused, flew up and hung mid-air as though he were awaiting a high-five.

Doctor Wen raised an eyebrow. 'Is everything okay Mr. Bartkowski?'

'Yes,' Edik said as if swallowing vomit. 'Fine. Okay. Yes,' he continued, focusing all his efforts on fighting his right hand with his left, trying to grasp the slip. He was only mildly aware of Doctor Wen's concern as his hands battled each other and eventually lefty triumphed with a deft slap and grab, stuffing the crumpled paper into the pocket of his jeans.

He rose, rubbing the soreness away with his left hand. The right seemed to be cooperating now. He made his apologies and departed fumbling the door handle on his way out.

*

It was almost evening by the time he'd struggled home, the voices in his head screaming not to take the medicine. But Edik wanted his body back, wanted to be in control once more. After clanging through his front door, he staggered to the sink, legs twisting every which way they could to slow him down.

'Stop it!' he shouted. 'It's happening, whether you like it or not.' *I'm insane. This infection has sent me mad. It's the lack of food, water...*

Please, said Muse, its voices echoing in his head as if it were hollow. *You're not mad. Have mercy. We'll allow you to eat a little. We'll look after you better.*

'No,' said Edik, reaching for the cupboard above the sink and taking out a glass.

Think of your writing. You like writing, don't you? Edik ignored the voices, *his* voices, as he wrestled the glass to the tap and filled it. *You're nothing without us,* the voices screeched so loud and so suddenly he felt as though his head would split.

He dropped the glass in the sink, losing power over both hands and stepped back wishing for nothing more than the searing headache to ease off. *Nothing*, said Muse, *you are ours!*

From where he found the energy and resolve, Edik wasn't certain but there it was. Those words were enough. He straightened and said aloud, 'No. It's my body, my mind. Not yours.'

In swift fluid movements he darted back to the sink, filled the glass, popped the antibiotic capsule on his tongue and washed it down. His head felt like a log split by an axe. His vison blurred, dropping to his knees as the pain became too much. He passed out on the kitchen floor.

It was good to be out, to be in the sun and feel the fresh air on his cheeks again. Edik sat on a bench enjoying a morning croissant and coffee whilst people watching in the hope of getting some inspiration for a follow up to his bestseller.

Coming towards him along the path was an elderly lady with huge oval sunglasses and bouffant blond hair, walking the kind of dog that seemed more suited to being carried than its frantic wiggling walk.

Beyond her, on the river, local boating teams drew back and forth along shady waters where willows draped themselves like yogis stretching out their spines.

Usually, when he reread his first draft, he would find a few characters that lacked depth and before all this business with the bacteria, he had often sat by the river in the morning waiting for inspiration to strike him.

Edik only noticed he was at the end of the croissant when he bit his fingers. He laughed and stood, sipped what remained of his takeout coffee and tossed the paper cup into the bin beside the bench. Standing was easier since he'd got his strength back and Doctor Wen had been pleased with his recovery. His body was his own again and that pleased him more than anything.

Inspiration seemed not to be showing its face by the river so Edik decided he'd go down town to his usual haunt, Helluo Librorum, a bookish café where he always managed to think of something.

The name was Latin for "devourer of books" and Flo, the owner, had said she almost chose *Tinea* which also meant "head worm" in Latin, or something like that. She was thinking something like bookworm or inspiration, but a nurse friend told her it just made her think of fungal skin infections. So, Flo had decided against the name, she'd told him with a snort.

Edik liked Flo, and her café, and had been a frequent patron before he'd taken ill, regularly attending the writers' circle there every Wednesday evening. Maybe it was the scent of the coffee she used or the muffins she made. Who knew? It never seemed to fail to lure inspiration out of its hiding place and into his mind where he would snare it.

Edik Bartkowski stopped dead in the street all of a sudden struck by a thought; he hadn't been able to concentrate recently, not since... *Muse?* he called out with his mind.

Nothing.

Closing his eyes, he tried harder. *Muse?*

Still nothing, no ideas but the ramblings of his mind. He looked around the street in the manner of a suspicious sheep and whispered, 'Muse?' but nothing happened.

A cold sweat formed across his brow as he stood on the pavement in the middle of town, people passing by too absorbed in their phones to notice. Either checking their social media or talking into the air it seemed, where they were actually speaking into their—

'—headphones!' The shout from Edik only drew a few curious glances, yet no one seemed perturbed by his sudden outburst.

In desperation, Edik rifled through his battered leather shoulder bag until he found his headphones, untangled them and plugged them into his phone and ears. Now he could call out to Muse and folk would no doubt suppose he was just trying to summon some app or something.

From that spot on the pavement all the way to Helluo Librorum, Edik called aloud to Muse. By the time he arrived at the café he was a bag of nerves and had forgotten the pleasure he'd taken from finally being out the house and was more concerned that he'd unwittingly destroyed the very thing that had honed his concentration. He hadn't been mad with sickness after all. The voices weren't the symptoms, they were something else.

'Where have you gone?' he asked in vain. 'Where are you? Muse, are you there? Hello? Hello?' As he stood with his back to the café, commuters passed by unaware he was talking to himself. Traffic moaned, caught in the morning rush.

'Hello? Muse? Please answer me.' His voice was

weak, catching in his throat and he felt desperate tears pressing behind his eyes as he saw his trilogy dreams swirling down the toilet.

I'm over-reacting. It's just writer's block Edik. Come on. You wrote and drafted a novel in five days and drafted the follow up, give yourself a break. But he found no solace in his thoughts.

The café, he thought and turned with renewed hope. He would order an Americano and a dark chocolate muffin, sit back and wait for inspiration to...

It was gone.

The café windows were whitewashed, the sign taken down and the crumpled notice plastered to the inside of the glass read: "New store coming soon."

In sudden despondence, Edik turned his back on the café and plodded home calling longingly to Muse both with mouth and mind.

That evening, Edik conducted a little research. He'd already found the reason why Helluo Librorum closed as he'd had Flo's phone number; he had been thinking about asking her on a date but then he'd taken ill and become a shut-in.

She'd sounded ashamed when she told him she was closed down on hygiene grounds and that she hadn't intended to make people ill with her muffins. Edik thought against mentioning he had taken ill too, wishing not to hurt her feelings.

Flo also informed him that if it was inspiration he was looking for he should contact Ellen, another previous regular and part of the writers' circle. She'd just scored a book deal and seemed brimming with so many ideas that even she said she was in excess of them. Edik ended the call with the usual polite words but put his phone down with chilling realisation.

The voice in my head... The bacteria?

After that he waded through junk on the internet panning for gold. He'd found an interesting study in the field of Neurochemistry about flow state and how the brain produced certain chemicals like the neurotransmitters serotonin and noradrenaline and how they increased a person's concentration and focus.

What spooked him most was that noradrenaline could cause high blood pressure. *Hadn't Doctor Wen said my blood pressure was high?* He certainly had been acutely focused on his writing over the previous weeks too.

A little more digging took him into the realm of Gut Science, something he'd never heard of before and he found an interesting theory as yet unproved. It sounded like quackery but Edik was desperate and emailed a Doctor Król who'd written a paper titled: "Your Microbiome is You: How Bacteria Control Our Thoughts."

Two days passed before Edik grew too impatient and frustrated to even spread jam on his morning toast and instead searched in a mad whirlwind of furling arms for the scrap of paper on which he'd scrawled Doctor Król's contact details.

His newly papered front room looked like a bombsite by the time he located it and was sitting in the middle of the mess on the floor waiting for Doctor Król to pick up.

A lady, who Edik assumed to be Król's assistant, answered after a few rings. When Edik asked to speak directly to the doctor, the assistant, who eventually gave her name as Lisa, told him she'd get Doctor Król to call him back and hung up before he could leave his number.

Edik waited for two more days. In that time, he finished decorating his flat in a hope the work would distract his racing mind and burn some of his excess energy. He'd recovered from the bacterial infection, his skin glowed, he had flesh on his bones again and his hair had regained its healthy sheen. Yet he'd give it all up to have Muse back again.

He hadn't written anything, not a word since he'd taken the antibiotics. Since he'd *killed* his own muse. The stupidity he felt for not having connected the dots haunted him.

At his last check-up with Doctor Wen he'd asked where she'd sent his stool sample, plotting in the back of his mind how he'd retrieve it. He also read about faecal implants and instead of disgust, was surprised to find himself devising ways he'd perform the procedure on himself once he'd got his sample—*his* muse—back again.

The ancient Chinese had called it "yellow soup", and even that didn't seem repulsive as he imagined what it would taste like.

Later on in the week, after harassing Doctor Król's assistant every day, the good doctor finally took his call but Edik's excitement was dashed as soon as she had begun to speak. Doctor Król asked so many questions, 'Why are you calling? Who do you work for? Which tabloid?'

Once he'd softened her mood with talk of their shared Polish heritage, she became a little more amiable, but not by much and told him that since publishing her research she'd been ridiculed in the papers and shunned by most of her peers.

Edik slumped, deciding not to tell her he was a writer and certainly not that he had previously been talking to the bacteria in his gut which had given him special concentrative powers and helping him with plot lines. There was only ever one way *that* conversation would go.

'But could bacteria affect your concentration?' he asked. He heard Doctor Król sigh on the other end of the line and thought he'd pushed his luck too far, but to his surprise, she spoke.

'It's complicated,' she said, 'but bear with me. Your gut is home to all sorts of bacteria, which makes up your microbiome. It's like a little ecosystem. Serotonin is the key Mr. Bartkowski.'

'Yeah, your paper said that ninety percent of the body's serotonin is produced in the gut.'

'That's right,' she said, a little snort just audible over the phone. Impressed he'd read her paper perhaps? Edik wasn't sure. 'There's evidence that microbes in the gut use this neurotransmitter to communicate with the vagus nerve thus sending messages to the brain. This could manifest as craving certain foods for example, something the bacteria like. To put it in plain terms.'

Edik thought about that for a few seconds and said, 'Even craving concentration?'

Doctor Król laughed, 'There's no proof of course, but...'

Edik hung on her words, waiting for what he wanted to hear but nothing came. '...but flow state increases serotonin and dopamine, noradrenaline, endorphins...' he rattled the list off in desperation. 'They're addictive, right?'

The doctor laughed again. 'I'm impressed Mr. Bartkowski, you've certainly done your homework. But that's in the field of Neurochemistry, I specialise in bacteria.'

'But the brain could become addicted, right?' he pressed.

'Scientists prefer the term "autotelic" Mr. Bartkowski. And yes, such chemicals if released in great quantities could induce autotelic behaviour. It's interesting that you mention that connection...' her voice trailed off in thought.

Edik felt he'd said too much. Perhaps she'd tumble

to what he was thinking, research the area more, get a hold of the muse bacteria. He panicked, thanked her for her time in a clumsy manner and hung up hastily.

He stared at the notes he'd made over the past few days and crossed out her name. At the bottom of the list was his other lead from Doctor Wen.

'Kings College London?' he said aloud, falling back in his seat, glum and hopeless. *How the hell can I retrieve my sample?*

Staring at his laptop brought no inspiration and he thought how easily inspiration had come with the bacteria swimming around in his gut.

Realising he was thirsty, Edik wandered into his newly fitted kitchen. Whilst he stood waiting for his coffee to brew his mind drifted to the Wednesday writers' group and how he missed chatting to Matt, Felica, Gwen, Darren, Ellen...

'Ellen!' He jumped up from the kitchen counter as he shouted the name. *Flo said Ellen was full of ideas, that Ellen—*

He was dialling her in a heartbeat. *I need that bacteria. I need it.*

'Hello?' A woman's voice, it sounded distant, thin.

'Ellen?'

She confirmed it was her with a weak 'uh-huh' and Edik reminded her who he was. They played pleasantry tennis asking about each other until he managed to wheedle a morning coffee out of her in the guise of a writers' meet, with one stipulation; he wanted to meet her at her place.

'Sure, that would be great,' said Ellen. Edik was surprised it had been so easy, imagining she'd think it weird, a little creepy and out of the blue but reminded himself how he'd found it nigh on impossible to leave his flat when he had a gut full of the bacteria.

He thanked her, hung up and sighed relief. *Now, how do I get a sample?* He also thought he'd keep calling it *sample* as it sounded less creepy and weird and more like a science project.

Pressing the doorbell again, this time holding it a little longer, Edik wondered if Ellen had forgotten their coffee morning or even had second thoughts and was ignoring him. He back stepped down the path to look up at the first-floor window he vaguely remembered being hers. The party had been a while ago and as usual, he'd been a little squiffy.

The net curtain there finally twitched when he'd almost given up. A fresh electric excitement buzzed through him and he patted his leather shoulder bag, mentally going through the items he'd packed; a lunchbox with a firm lid, latex gloves, a teaspoon and a few packets of laxative.

After Ellen buzzed him in, Edik climbed the stairs to her flat in trepidation, battling with himself. He felt sullied and strange. A sick feeling of wrongness bubbled in his gut and he imagined he was some kind of serial killer plotting the deed. Yet what worried him most was the thrill it gave him. *It won't hurt her,* he told himself. *It's just a laxative, that's all.*

Her door was already open a crack when he'd made his way along the landing to her flat. He knocked the door out of curtesy which creaked with the force of his knuckles and announced he was entering.

Ellen's flat was much like his had been when he'd been infected. Dark, disordered, the faint smell of socks. Ellen sat in the glow of her laptop screen at her cluttered desk.

'Hey,' said Ellen, not even glancing up, fingers fluttering across keys.

'Hey,' said Edik in return. *Good, she's oblivious, she hasn't made the connection.* He looked around, not a coffee pot in sight. Good, he'd offer to make it, all the better.

Strolling over to her, they exchanged further greetings and questions showing vague interest in each other's lives but Edik avoided asking her directly about her sudden inspired surge as of late, nor did she offer any insight.

He sat himself on the soft couch which swallowed him hungrily. Around it were hastily scribbled notes scattered like autumn leaves, chewed hardbacks and paperbacks with spines cracked and arched. All strewn about, casualties of the bacteria's thirst for endorphins.

'Coffee?' Edik squeaked, clapping his hands together, fidgeting with nerves.

'Oh sorry, I—' Ellen started to rise from her seat though her eyes never left that screen. *Has she even looked at me?* Panic took him and he exploded from the couch to his feet.

'No!' he blurted, a little too loud. Ellen looked up then. Suspicion? He prayed not. His mind stumbled over what to say, some way to rescue the moment. 'I mean, no, allow me. You look like you're in the flow. I don't want to—'

'—thanks,' she said, already retaking her seat, 'that's sweet of you. Coffee's in the top left cupboard, sugar too if you want it. The cafetière is next to the kettle. Just milk for me.' She was fixated on her screen again, fingers tapdancing with gay abandon.

Edik found his way round the dishevelled kitchen and out of interest peeked in Ellen's fridge finding exactly what he expected; nothing but condiments and a furry chunk of cheese.

Good, Edik thought as he opened his bag to which he'd clung since entering Ellen's flat; not that she'd noticed. He retrieved his gastrointestinal espionage kit, glancing with edgy eyes over his shoulder every ten seconds.

He dumped a double dose of laxative into Ellen's coffee and added a little milk as requested, pleading to which ever god or power was listening that she wouldn't notice the taste. He then turned to his secret weapon, something he'd considered whilst plotting the whole thing.

It had occurred to him that she may grow suspicious if she suddenly developed diarrhoea during his visit and might even cotton on to his plot.

He took the small cream cakes out of their plastic box and plated them up nicely, two for him and two for her, thinking that if she did start asking questions, he could blame the cream as it would be more likely to upset a stomach than coffee. After he placed them on her desk with a kind smile, he took up his place on the couch and waited.

And waited...

'Don't forget your coffee,' said Edik, sweating copiously. The anticipation was killing him. He'd adjusted his sitting position who knows how many times; legs crossed, uncrossed, casually draped on the arm of the couch, he even sat in lotus position in the hope it would calm him the hell down.

Drink the bloody coffee Ellen!

As though their minds were wirelessly connected, Ellen unconsciously reached for her mug, fingertips brushing the handle lightly before she snapped her hand back to the keypad. *Some sudden inspiration no doubt,* thought Edik jealously.

A couple more heart pulling false moves later and finally Ellen took a long thirsty draught of her coffee and to Edik's surprise, nibbled the cream cake. He surrendered to the couch and gave his watch a sly glance. *How long for a double dose to kick in?*

Edik heard Ellen's stomach churn, even over the tapping of her fingers. A hellish gurgling, he imagined it twisting her gut so much even her muse wouldn't be able to convince her to stay seated and type. 'Oh. Sorry,' she said, standing.

Spluuur-ggghch-loooock!

She crumpled in half clutching her belly with her left hand whilst still typing with her right.

Guurrr-puuuur-lopcchhh!

Her knees twisted together and she almost left her desk yet her right hand would not budge from the computer. *Geez, this one's stubborn,* thought Edik as he watched with fascination.

'Are you okay Ellen?' He feigned concern so well that he'd even convinced himself he was worried.

'Er, yeah,' Gurlp-lug-arrr, 'I just—I think I—' Blurp-lac-cacacak. 'One minute,' she said and was gone, stumbling over this and that on route to the bathroom.

The noise that erupted from the bathroom was horrendous and when Ellen returned, she appeared dazed and a little off, face blushed pink with embarrassment. She made her apologies to which Edik insisted there was no need and that it was *he* who should apologise and vowed to never pick up reduced-price cream cakes again. Then, clutching his stomach, made out he was suffering from the same affliction and ran to the bathroom.

He paid a visit to his bag on the counter on the way, snatching up his sample kit and disappeared into her tiny bathroom, ensuring the door was locked.

The lid to the toilet was down but it didn't keep back the acrid rotten egg smell that lingered. Edik ignored it, intent on his prize and crossed his latex covered fingers as he lifted the lid up and smiled. Although she'd flushed, a little remained. Edik repeated the nurse's words, 'A small amount is all we need.'

He set to work.

When Edik returned home that night, he had one last meal before he put his head down for the night; a yellowish soup flavoured with a little cumin. He hoped the bacteria wouldn't mind the spice.

It had been an awful night, battling the urge to vomit and go to the toilet, but somehow Edik had proven very valiant in his efforts and was now grinning. His fingers flew over his keyboard and seemed to blur.

Write, said the voices he'd named Muse. The voices had been all too happy to assume such a name. Edik wrote, but it was not a story, not yet. Ellen had made a full recovery after her purge. Which had got Edik and the new muse thinking. Purging the competition of their concentration was certainly a curious opportunity only a fool would pass up.

So, he continued compiling the list of names of writers who had attended the last meeting at the café.

He was of the mind to give them a call, ask if they were well. If not, he'd pay them a visit and take care of them—out of the kindness of his own heart of course.

YOU WON'T EVEN KNOW

They said we wouldn't even know they were here. That's what they claimed when they arrived. 'We won't be a bother,' they told every world leader in each culture's native tongue. 'Here to observe, to collect data, nothing more,' they said.

That year the world turned on as usual.

From inside the skin of some of our own, amongst us, they spoke. 'It is required, don't worry about it.' They gave us a gift, a symbol of goodwill.

That year humanity took to the stars.

'Don't worry yourselves. It's natural. Trust our ancient knowledge of worlds,' they implored.

That year our best minds warned of our world warming and we did not listen.

'It will ease off and eventually cease. Just the cycle

of your world is all. You are too young, but we are ancient, we know,' they said.

That year the first of the domes went up over our cities.

'They are for your own safety. It's fine, the cycle is almost complete. Remain inside, let us risk ourselves out there. We are a hardy species. Don't fret,' they said.

That year the air outside grew thick and dark.

'It doesn't matter what the machines do. Your minds are not like ours. You wouldn't comprehend. Just work them dutifully and work them well. Trust in them and trust in us,' they said.

That year we finally lost our questioning nature.

They said we wouldn't even know they were here. 'We were wrong. The case is severe. Your world must be saved. We need the outside help,' they said.

That year more ships came. Then for the first time the world saw them, as they were, not wearing us. Now everyone knows they are here.

HOW PLASTIC IS THE
HUMAN MIND?

Animo News: Big Central. Breaking: Vagus, Police-
citizen altercation. One officer and six Organics injured.
Want mods? Can't afford extortionate prices? Old Doc's
modifications.

Teddy Mullen's arms ached. How long had it been
now? Ten, fifteen minutes? It was hard to be certain.
But then who could these days? With so much data
coursing through your head, images of the past,
present and an imagined future—time dissolved into
obscurity. You remembered things, sure, but could
you ever be sure it was *you* remembering or if they
were just data memories? Data memories fed to you
by an algorithm hungry for information. Hungry to
grow, to expand, to learn.

   Ted narrowed his eyes helping his ocular implants
fight the acid rain haze and neon glare meddling with
his sight. Evenings in Big Central had always been

rather jarring. Harsh primary coloured shards of light like shattered stained glass slicing your vision.

The handgun—the one staring him down with its lethal glare—was local enforcer issue, compact, black and sleek and rather nice to handle. Just like the one in his grasp.

How much longer are you gonna do this? Come on, put the gun down kid.

How she had acquired that sidearm was embarrassing. He'd not witnessed the altercation himself, however, it was clear that his partner, Velázquez, who was now writhing around on the rain slickened street, had misinterpreted the situation.

It was obvious, now, to his partner and the Organics scattered around the street, that this delicate girl wasn't all that delicate.

Velázquez though… come off it. Should've known better.

Mullen thought about how death always lingered a few steps behind when you walked the beat. He thought about his rabbit hutch apartment. He thought about the roof he risked his life to keep over his head. Over Nancy's head, and soon, his daughter's.

Will I even see my child born? Yes. He damn well would. Of that, he was adamant.

He kept his eyes narrowed.

His retinal implants worked hard to sharpen the shimmering silhouette of the girl. Fixed, his eyes not faltering. A direct line to the wet glint of hers reflecting back the fractured light of nightclubs, bars and biohacker joints.

Never look down the barrel. Never. Only one thing that's down there Ted.

No, never look *down* it.

The quiver in her eyes, even at this distance, betrayed the girl's mental state; the battle inside her head. The weapon, that dark steel emptiness at the edge of sight, wavering ever so slightly in porcelain white hands.

How old are you? Seventeen? Older? Come on… put it down. Do it. Come on. Please.

Commercial gene editing and biohacking was making it increasingly trickier to determine such arbitrary things as age and ethnic origin these days. Not that it mattered. A gun was a gun.

This clinched it. That desk he'd shied away from in favour of what he'd so naïvely viewed as *pure* police work looked damn appealing right now. He loathed working Vagus.

There was always *something*.

'Citizen!' he blasted over the whoop-whoop of his police pod's sirens. The girl's head jerked upward, the motion tugging at Mullen's gut feeling in a disagreeable way.

He primed himself, releasing his breath, allowing it

to mingle with the tainted city air.

No. Don't do it. He was pleading with the girl now. *Put the gun down.* Was he even on the girl's nexting feed? He wasn't sure, but he'd try anyhow.

Nexts were better than speech in such cases. Almost like thoughts. You could get into people's heads. But here, something seemed wrong. Something rang odd about her. Was it her mannequin attitude? The hinged gesture of her limbs when she had moved, maybe?

'We got a name?' he spoke from the corner of his mouth to any one of the officers that had coalesced about the unfolding drama.

A reply came, not his partner, but someone else. Mullen dared not move to see who. To flinch now could be catastrophic.

'Larn.'

Definitely not another cop.

He'd been on the Vagus beat long enough. He had file upon file warehoused in the annals of his digitally enhanced mind. Each and every one cross referenced and verified in a split-second. Before he could speak, to reason with this *Larn*, the stand-off ended.

A feather light twitch in the girl's index finger, imperceptible to the naked, unmodified, eye.

Not such a long night then.

*

A few weeks earlier…

Larn Baxter watched with impassive eyes as it rolled by in polychromatic streamers. The city's neon glow, rippled over the polished smart-glass windows of the taxi pod in laser-light caterpillars as it slipped through constricted streets. Citizens ducking in and out of shady buzz-joints and dubious back alley biohacking parlours, retinal implants enriching tumultuous heat shimmers spooling from yawning doors, meandering citizens shrouded in plastic against the rain like the seats of a brand-new pod fresh from the showroom.

Far too many people for her liking.

Compressed humanity, their shimmering electromagnetic auras, crowns of pulsing chakra radiation. Connected, hooked up. Each and every one of them, bar the odd remaining few, the Orgs. Tunes dropped directly into their heads, they nodded like galley slaves locked into the beat of the drum, at the same instance, communicating with thousands of others, mind to mind. The magic of mindreading coldly dissected and reassembled by science and technology, up-linking every willing soul to Animo, the wireless AI network, connected the remaining pockets of civilization that had survived Calamity.

Much like Larn.

Calamity, however, was a mere history lesson to her. A second-hand memory with the attachments and footnotes of others. Despite that, the memory felt like hers. So well planted in her head, embedded and engrained. Reminding her—reminding them all—to be good a citizen.

Her ride jerked and shuddered adjusting to the slow trudge of coagulated downtown streets, merging with surgical precision into the plethora of pedestrians and ambling robotic food dispensers. The taxi pod became one with the undulating masses. Like a mistrusting child, Larn scrutinised the outside world. She strained against her impulse to command the taxi pod to turn back. To retreat home where she knew she would be safe with her classic movies, retro computer games and cyberfriends. The allure was intense.

She hated crowds, despite the hush of them.

The silence unnerved her the most. All those people, but hardly any noise save the shuffling of feet, the rustle of plastic shower-proofs and the rasping and lurching coughs pulled from polluted lungs. She settled back into the wipe-clean vinyl seat of the pod and began to casually cycle through her ocular implant's visual spectrum. That seemed to bring her back down, soothe that old anxiety which followed her around like a needy pup.

In an instant, her world switched to blood orange hues tumbling from the warm doorways of shop fronts, street lamps and neon signs. Skimming through the spectrums was a coping mechanism, she was well aware of that.

When are you going to sort it out? her mind jibed.

There's nothing to sort out.

Sure there is. Come on. You know it. Your parents know it. Dex *knows it. You wouldn't want to disappoint* him *now, would you?*

Shut up!

She flicked through more filters, shifting from one radiant world to the next until the voices gave up. The relief was bitter-sweet, but a relief nonetheless. Ever since she had upgraded her vision, Larn had used it as a distraction. Applying filters to life with a mere thought. She wished the world an emerald green. Another wish and the street was an eerie wash of electric blue. A sunlit alien ocean. The people fish, the shops a neon reef.

Anything to spirit her away.

But Big Central *was* like an alien world to her. Reality, a grim acid eroded city. A masked-up populous terrified of the particulate matter skulking in the air. A sea of plastic hoods musing black market implants, always looking for the next modification.

It had got worse too.

The previous year saw a tremendous rise in body-tech mods and a subsequent rise in cost. Animo's perpetual data stream compelling citizens to quench their addiction seeking out cheaper, but lower quality modifications. People's ethics and morals were slipping. The concept of "human" was slipping. All of it trickling away down into the already burdened underground veins of the city.

Implants. Implants. Implants.

Retinal, cochlear, neural; Vagus street had everything you never knew you desired.

'Just here.' Larn's own voice struck her as outlandish. The exertion of speaking a chore to underused vocal chords.

You need to stop that. Her father's voice. *You need to use your mouth sweetie. Stop!*

'Stopping,' said the pod in flawless imitation of her mother's voice. Larn barely even remembered giving the pod permission to appropriate the samples from her data files. That sort of thing happened so fast. It was hard to recall the exact instant.

You need to be careful sweetie. Her father's voice, floating round her head. *Taking information. It's always taking information.*

It? It… who's it exactly?

Animo. Animo is always there. You should have stayed organic. I should have put my foot down.

No. I need this. It's just normal

He always had been old-fashioned.

'You have arrived at your destination.' Her mother's voice again now. 'West Vagus street. Air quality index reading 895. PM2.5—extremely unhealthy. Be sure to wear a breather if you have non-modified lungs. It is not suitable for Organic citizens to be outside for longer than ten minutes. Take care and enjoy your evening—sweetie.'

The intonation was choppy, the data added in a sloppy manner and the endearment term oddly tagged on. The illusion ruined. Cheap AI. Larn ignored the information. Her lungs had long been proofed against the fetid air. She made no remark, no goodbye as the pod's gullwing door juddered upward. It got stuck halfway forcing Larn to duck out. She immediately found herself inserted amongst the mass of autonomously rolling vending machines, hobbling commercial-bots, and shuffling citizens. Police drones hovered above in clouds like the mosquitos in the humid summers.

A commercial-bot caught Larn's eyes in a bewildered double-take. Instead of catchphrases marketing recycled food or cheap mods, the blinking light screen read: RISE. The thick bold typesetting glimmered hypnotically as the bot sauntered about with no obvious direction in mind.

She blinked, convinced she was seeing things and the message was gone, replaced with the picture of a cute child about to indulge in a recycled burger. Larn swallowed away the sour memory of taste that had manifested at the nauseating thought of recycled meat—it never failed to make her heave. The piquant scent of real grilled meat came along on the clammy cloud of life that hung over Vagus. Cumin, caraway and fennel. An agreeable veil of eastern spices chasing away the unpleasant memories of faux food. The bot's subliminal message was already lost in the undulating sea of useless information that was her mind.

Lost, but not gone.

Larn made her way through a mix of organic and modified humans. For the unenhanced eye, it was impossible to tell an Organic apart from a Modified. Labourers, tourists, teenagers, shop owners; the distinction was generally a subtle one.

Whether a surgical implant, a custom-grown organ or a genetic mod, most people were subtle and clandestine about them—except for Techsters. A dazzling throng of them prattled past Larn, the loudest people on the street. Peacocks proudly sporting dermal lights pulsing beneath their skin. Vagus street was *the* place to be.

Larn's heart pounded as they went by.

In a flush of embarrassment, she receded into the crowd a little, pulling her hood over her face. She recognised them from college, had observed them from a safe distance without their knowing, dreaming of being like them.

You're so dull. She imagined them saying.

What makes you even think we'd give you a second look?

You have character sweetie. Don't listen to them.

Thanks dad.

They passed on by, a neon buzz, oblivious to her presence. She was, after all, just another pallid face blending in with the masses—nothing special. Larn's own implants lay hidden beneath her skin, and deep within the tissue of her brain. Inconspicuous additions to her human form. That narked her every day, living in a world where everyone else seemed to be free to express themselves.

Her Direct Neural Interface had been installed for her fifteenth birthday, but her father had forbidden any visible 'aesthetic implants' as he always called them.

She'd bugged her parents relentlessly for her DNI. Everyone in school had had one long before her. She'd persevered and they eventually caved in. Her mom had reasoned with her father, said that she'd be disadvantaged without it. Larn had instantly synched her DNI with the house and the city's Animo Network.

With Wi-Fi directly linked to her brain, she could hear cyberspace. The freedom was overwhelming. Suddenly she could fly. Since then, the cortical plasticity of her brain had long adapted to it, learned how to understand and master the enormous invasion of images, sound files and Neural Text Messages known as nexts.

It snowballed after that.

She had weakened her father's resolve. For her sixteenth year, she'd had her retinal implants. For her seventeenth year it was a deluxe Animo update. And now, for her eighteenth…

'Hey Larn! Hey!'

Over the hushed meandering crowd, the shout rang clear. Heads turned in reflex rather than actual interest. Passive gazes searching through habit rather than intent, then back to whatever had been captivating them within the confines of their own minds.

Dex, Larn nexted, *sorry I'm late I—*

'Come on Larn,' said Dex, 'speak with your mouth.'

You know I can't, Dex. Come on. Don't make me, she sent. She loathed the rudimentary clumsiness of speech. Nexting was so much more. Not just internal text, but feelings too. Vigour clung to each word as it was thought, the network shuffling it along. Like telepathy, really.

After pulling his way through the crowd, Dex stopped just in front of her. 'You know I'm old-school,' he said.

Larn screwed up her face, but said nothing.

Dex sighed. *Fine, happy now?*

She grinned.

He grabbed her by the hand and hauled her into the shuffling silence. Stealing through the crowds along Vagus, erupting into an unanticipated clearing where a commotion had gathered onlookers.

'Cleanse yo plastic mind. Embrace oomanity. We al come from de Earth itself!' barked a hoary guy in rough Outer Ring speak.

The ambling crowd observed in that gawkish way rubber-neckers observed a car accident. Not a soul heckled him, every one of them too wrapped up in their digital minds, linked up to Animo. Vacant expressions, not really taking part in life, but merely witnessing it through a stream of images, tags and comments.

Larn *heard* him though. She alone *was* listening.

His wild eyes seized hers.

Stranded in his madness, his look lured her in. Deeper, deeper…

Rise!

'What?' she said, confused. Did the word come from his lips or from her head? Dex paused mid-stride, regarding Larn in puzzlement.

'Don't be taintin yo skin,' spoke the crazy guy. 'Don't be pollutin yo body. We organic children of Gaia. You! Why? Why destroy yoself child?'

He started for her, but Dex was already yanking her away, back into the crowd.

'What's up with you Larn?'

I—I thought he… Never mind.

'Whatever.' He shrugged. 'Come on! And speak with your mouth.'

He's right sweetie. Her mother's voice. *Speak with your mouth. He's a good guy, that Dex. Would make a great boyfriend. Not like those tech-heads, techsters… whatever you call them.*

No. Just no. Dex is a friend.

Boyfriend?

No.

You do spend a lot of time together. Why not make it official? He's a nice guy.

That's why. I don't like nice guys… I—

—like bad boys? Her own mind cut in. *Like you'd have the nerve to ever look one in the eyes.*

Shut up. Just, just—

She blinked her vision to black and white and flattened the image. The lack of colour and depth seemed to work; drowned out the chatter. She had to focus more on where she was going, it was like walking through the pages of her old noir comic books.

So long as it worked…

The masses of people they had sought cover in eventually began to thin out as they danced their way along Vagus and soon there was room to breathe, the shadier nooks of Vagus opened up to them.

Larn glanced around anticipating a mugging or some seedy character to try something on. Light clusters flickered hypnotically like luminous glass eggs, painting the place with intermittent blackness, save the low-lit windows where half naked men and women swayed in seductive rhythm.

Where are we Dex?

Beckoning eyes, and bodies heavily modified with robotic legs or arms seducing the mod-curious, danced to an unheard beat. Larn could feel that anxiety flushing her body again. She had never ventured this far down Vagus before.

'It's a surprise,' said Dex, his voice electric with excitement.

You know how I feel about surprises, she sent.

He absorbed the next in a flash. Subconsciously soaking up the words displayed in his vison along with her anxiety. He spun and smiled, hoping it would chase away her fear and said, 'You'll like this one.' He thought, then added, 'Don't worry. I'm here.'

Larn smiled timidly.

A young girl caught Larn's eye as they wandered along. It was like looking in a mirror. Larn blinked the world back to technicolour to get a good look at her sat in the vivid buzz of a graffitied doorway. Knees up by her ears, tags and erratic scrawls crowding her. Larn came over giddy all of a sudden. The graffiti seemed to swirl and reconfigure itself, right there on the wall. Was it her software? Had she somehow changed a setting by accident with her habitual filter flicking? Or a virus? No, her neural firewall was up.

The writing on the wall rethreaded and wound around like a nest of serpents. Serpents forming something with their undulating bodies. A word. A word as of yet unformed but Larn already knew what it would say.

RISE.

She blinked and in an instant the graffiti snapped back to normal.

'Larn?' Dex's voice was distant. *Larn!*

Sorry, she sent. 'I mean—sorry. I—'

'You okay? You seem a bit twitchy tonight.'

She considered telling him, but thought better of it. 'No, I'm fine,' she said and looked back at her doppelganger. The once bright colours of the girl's clothes were now a faded, a grubby reminder that she had probably had a home and money once. The desperate urge to do something, to help the girl welled up within Larn, imagining herself on the cold wet street, a torn piece of cardboard with "For mods" hastily scribbled in fading lime green lipstick next to a nervously chewed paper cup; a couple of dirty old credits tossed in it.

Paying more attention to the girl, rather than to where she was going, Larn didn't notice the buzz from her proximity app and tumbled into Dex. She was about to berate him when his beaming smile stole her irritation. His arms opened upwards framing a huge pink neon sign it read: Old Doc's Modifications.

'Ta-da!'

What? This, *is it?* Larn sent.

Dex's arms dropped along with his shoulders

hanging on a lanky frame, *C'mon, you know what this is?* he nexted.

Larn shrugged. *Biohacker joint. A really low-grade one too Dex.*

He turned to her, obviously more excited than she was. *Yeah—Well… We're students. What do you expect? Anyway, you said that after we turned eighteen we'd both get hacked. Like, properly this time. Something everyone can see. I'm nineteen next month Larn. Nineteen.*

Head hung low, she searched the pavement, thinking about what her father would say. *None of those aesthetic modifications. Keep it subtle sweetie. You'll thank me for it when you're older.*

No, I won't.

You will Larn. Come on, listen to your dad for once. Come on…

C'mon Larn. What do you say? sent Dex.

She considered the Mods she had passed earlier; the group from college. She considered her father's words, what her mother would say…

Well? Dex twitched with impatient energy. *I'm getting my hands upgraded, I think. I'm not totally sure yet—there's so much to choose from. What about you?*

A few quiet moments passed. Only the depressing shuffle of lost souls shambling around the dark end of Vagus were audible.

I don't know. Maybe… Biohacks are serious things, not

like surreptitious implants, nexted Larn.

I know.

They actually *cut parts off.*

I know…

Actual *body parts Dex!*

Yeah, yeah. But it's totally safe. C'mon, everyone's doing it. Besides, if you don't like it you can just get your hands and stuff regenerated.

But that's expensive...

Dex shrugged. Yeah, but it's a fix, right? So, what's your problem? Come on...

He had a point.

Somewhere in her defiant teenage mind, it made sense. Limb regeneration technology was available at both hospitals and private companies. And if everybody was doing it then… Not just the kids in her year at college, but popular faces in the media too. Fewer people seemed to be bothered by it. Her dad worried about her getting mods because back when he was a kid those kind of people got a hard time from Orgs. Things had changed—sort of.

She imagined how her hair would look long, short, shaved, orange, green and blue, as they climbed up the grubby white steps to the bio-hacker joint.

A scalp mod would *be cool,* she sent. *You sure this place is okay Dex?* Larn knew she was slipping back into her anxiety again. Second thoughts looming like the dark and dangerous under-the-bed monsters of her childhood.

Yeah, it'll be fine, Dex reassured her, waving his hands in that dismissive way he always did when making life changing decisions. *Seriously, don't worry. Zem was here last week. She got her whole left arm upgraded. Real smart.*

They both made their way across the scuffed chequered floor. Discarded cigarettes, empty vape cartridges and pseudo-stims were strewn across it. She wrinkled her nose at the state of the place. They paused at the reception desks—or what passed for them. Three silver check-plated plinths. Worn-out, old, box shaped desktop computers sat there. Facades probably. Larger than most available on the market nowadays. Antique shells, the tech inside undoubtedly up to spec. It added to the retro vibe the place had— or dive vibe.

Larn couldn't decide which.

A lanky old man—a relic himself—occupied the central desk like a greying spider.

With an apprehension he wouldn't admit to Larn, Dex approached the antediluvian proprietor. Possibly Old Doc himself. His goggle-masked eyes set deeply below a wrinkly frown of bristly white eyebrows, engrossed in whatever it was he was doing.

A patchy white beard clung to his chin like a long-forgotten cobweb. His long spidery fingers dancing across the clackerty keyboard below. Larn found it hard to ignore the melted plastic and detergent ozone which hung around him. She stood a little behind Dex, her nose covered with a hand. Her nasal filters protected against particulate matter, but not against bad smells.

'Yeah?' croaked the old guy, not looking up, not needing to. He was most likely jacked into all the security feeds in his parlour. He continued in broad Ringer speak, 'New hands, right?'

'Yeah. For me,' said Dex, unfazed by the old man's clairvoyant talents. Dex had been openly broadcasting his thoughts via the shop's Wi-Fi since they had entered after scanning the QR code at the door. The old man had some examples already prepared.

'Upgrades today. Hands, two for one deal.'

He spluttered out a phlegmy cough-laugh as he cranked the screen round for Dex. It creaked brittle and plastic, as if it would break.

'Magnetic finger tips. Read those electromagnetic fields at a wave of an and,' the old guy laughed and hacked out his sales pitch. Pinching a stim stick from his top right breast pocket he motioned to Larn, 'What about yo girl there?'

I'm not his girl, she sent.

He snorted, took a deep drag on the stim stick, it hissed as he drained it then tossed it. He lifted his goggles for a peek at Larn with an organic gaze. *One of those huh? Shy types. Maybe yo wan install a new personality app eh?* Even his thoughts felt like a Ringer's.

He stooped down to rummage amongst grey plastic storage crates marked "Norg Technologies" that lay strewn at his feet. His spine and ribs pressed through his skin-tight whites like the husk of a long dead and dried up insect. He popped back up with a sealed foil package and spoke with his mouth, 'Got de code ere. Unique. Call em splitz. Does as it sez. Splits yo personality. Hacks yo mind right. Yo wanna be life of de party? This does it instant like. One oondred credits.' He flashed perfect synthetic teeth.

Larn mused the little packet, scrunched her face and turned away. *Just a scalp mod thanks.*

'As yo wish it lil miss.'

The old guy pulled his goggles back down turning his attention to Dex who was judiciously perusing the selection on the screen. He edged forward—a little too close.

'Yo only av two ands there fella,' he said dryly, breath like sweaty warm ham. 'What it be then ma boy?'

'New hands,' said Dex barely containing his excitement.

'Yeah, I get that. Which model?' said the doc, spinning the console back around and pulling up a bio-med form.

'HND701/5, please.'

'Nice, nice. Yo av good taste yoong man. Polyethylene resin skeleton. Fire retardant dermal job too. Yo know yo can shape metal with yo bare ands with these. Yo an engineer boy? It'll cost yo more if no.'

A bristly eyebrow raised like a porcupine preparing to defend itself.

'Nah, not yet. Engineering student,' Dex said, hoping that would suffice.

The old guy frowned, 'Yo got ID? I don't wanna no mod-cops breakin down me doors. I run a respectable joint.'

Dex snorted. *Yeah right.* He checked his balance online. It was low, but just enough. He immediately transmitted his student number and personal ID. Enough to satisfy the old man it seemed.

'Okay, got it. Two thousand credits then,' the doc tapped in the code and sealed the deal. 'What about her?'

Just the scalp mod, Larn nexted to Dex. She cast her eyes to the ground, staring at her plain, mediocre boots.

'Scalp mod for her,' said Dex. The next part he transmitted on a private frequency, *And one of those Splitz too—for her.*

The old doc returned the request with a wry smile. *Sneaky implants cost extra,* he sent.

Dex hid his frown behind the best blank expression he could manage, *How much extra?*

Another five oondred credits.

Dex considered the amount for a second or two. It seemed a little steep, but then, he would be happy to part with the credits to see Larn come out of her shell a little. He would have to dip into his college savings, but she was worth it. It was her birthday after all.

She just needs a push is all. His own mind gently whispered. *Just a nudge. She'll thank you for it.*

Will she though?

Sure. Why not. You've seen how she looks at those guys at college. Not much of a best friend if you can't help her out, are you?

Dex looked at her, then the doc and forwarded the credits immediately. The old guy smiled and extended a long skeletal arm, 'Have a seat lil miss, I'ma do im first.' He stood. All seven feet of him unfolding in an unhurried fashion that grated against Dex's buzzing anticipation. He glided from the crowded plinth to the rear of the boutique.

'Step in,' he crooned, then called to someone behind Larn and Dex.

The curvaceous young woman was sat with her eyes closed, seemingly asleep. Dex assumed she must be watching a movie or something. The old boy hollered again and the woman slowly opened her eyes. She took a minute to adjust herself back to reality, stood, and sassed her way over to the leftmost plinth and made herself at home.

'Zaza, take care of de coostomers,' said the old man. And as an afterthought, 'No discounts or freebees for yo friends eh? Kes will tell me if yo do, won't yo Kes?'

'Sure,' replied a young techster who was currently engrossed in an old Gameboy. Both Dex and Larn had presumed him to be a patron, not an employee. Dex looked around at the people slumped around the place and laughed inwardly. Maybe they were all employees.

Animo Pop News: Norg Hansen, famed entrepreneur, socialite and CEO of Norg Technologies denies hacking claims. Modified Hansen claims no connection to recent government hacks which crippled Animo for fifteen minutes last week.

Mmmmmmmm! It's tasty, it's filling, it's recycled. It's every citizen's duty to conserve food. Reburger. Cheaper, better: recycled.

Larn sat lost in mashed up late '80s early '90s Manga videos playing on holo-screens scattered around the biohacker joint. She took her gaze from the anime momentarily to soak in the vibe of the waiting area a little more. Details she hadn't noticed before in her anxious haze began to creep in.

It had an antiquated atmosphere. A mishmash of early twentieth and twenty-first century kitsch. An eccentric mix of Cyber Synth Wave and Metal Step music played in the background whilst modified patrons lazed on a scrappy lime green couches, either engrossed in manga or lost in their digital minds.

Larn laughed inside at the absurdity of it all. So many subcultures, which would have seemed so odd to be bound together in such an intimate space back in their heyday, were now in perfect harmony. The hypocrisy of time.

She laughed again.

Yeah, she was a geek. But she didn't care, she loved those times. Had wished as a child that she had been born back then, certain it would've been better.

I'm done.

Dex's voice was unexpected, cutting into her mind. She stood and turned, still slightly lost in the warmness of childhood memories—real and imagined.

That was quick. She looked at his bagged hands. The skin wrinkled white like he'd been in the bath for far too long. 'How are they?' she asked aloud.

Dex grinned. A warm, glowing smile.

Larn could see he appreciated the gesture of *actually* speaking.

'Sore... I think.' He frowned. 'I mean—they *feel* fine, but I know they should be sore. There's a kinda tingling at the wrists.'

'Yo need to practise usin dem,' said the old guy

leaning in the doorway behind Dex. 'Software integration and neural recognition will take a while.'

He wandered to the desk at which Zaza was stood and muttered something Larn couldn't make out.

'Different brains, different time scales,' said the old Doc, looking up directly at Larn, then to Dex. 'If yo still av trouble after a monf, come an see me.'

The old doc looked to Larn again.

Rise up. Become.

'What?' she said aloud.

'I said, yo ready lil miss?'

It took Larn a second or two to realise what had happened. She glanced awkwardly at Dex, then the doc. *Yes, I'm ready.*

She motioned towards him, still a little nervous and confused. He ushered her into the room beyond, casting a final glance to Dex.

'Don't use yo ands for a month, yo av to let the bio-skin take. Okay?' He winked as he closed the doors.

Animo Financial News: Mods on the rise and Organics in decline. A new era?

Stream faster, next faster, live faster. Norg Technologies: programming your future faster.

Dex sat down in a bright yellow Pac-Man chair, the character seemingly swallowing him. He leant back. The cushions, tongue red, surrendered under his weight engulfing him. It was possibly the comfiest chair he'd ever sat in. Relaxed now, he suddenly became aware of a hunger so immense that he could even eat a recycled burger if he was given one.

His stomach bubbled at the thought of food.

He closed his eyes, summoned the location of all local restaurants and vendors. After a few seconds, he had made up his mind and ordered. The nexted response informed him the food would be about fifteen minutes. A sudden thought and he amended his delivery method to automated feeding. It would've been tricky otherwise. He settled back again into Pacman's mouth and became absorbed in the same mashed up anime that had amused his Larn, though she would have called it Manga, claiming she was even more old school than him.

Animo News headlines: Pollution levels to hit record breaking high. Norg Hansen to be investigated for hacking allegation. Org-Mod confrontation in Big Central East. Tensions between Modified and Organic citizens growing.

Mods, mods, mods. Cheap, affordable. Outer Ring, Big Central East

'Scalp implant took well,' said the doc as he came through the doors into the waiting room. He winked at Dex.

Larn stood there with her head all bandaged up like she had just stepped out of the shower and quickly wrapped a towel around it. 'Don't say a word,' she said, a little giggle escaped her lips.

Dex grinned in relief.

If he was honest with himself, he had been a little apprehensive. Concerned that she would notice the app and be angry with him. But she seemed unaware and the guilt diluted a little.

'How long for the bandages doc?' he asked on her behalf—an old habit.

'Give it a week,' he answered as he saw to a tall cyberpunk and his girlfriend. Her skinless bionic arm out on display—anodised green. The same shade as her boyfriend's hair. Dex nodded, smiled at Larn and they both made for the exit.

'So... How's the head?' said Dex as they stepped out onto the busy street mingling with the almost silent crowds.

'Fine. He gave me plenty of painkillers—can't wait to see what it's like. How're your hands now?'

'Yeah, they're good. Kinda weird not using them. I'm like you. Wanna try em out.'

But if he was honest, he had almost forgot about his hands. He was stunned. Larn was talking with her mouth. For as long as he had known her, she had always hated speaking out loud.

But now, as they strolled around checking out the clubs, she seemed relaxed. She had even started walking differently—sexy. From what he could tell, she hadn't noticed the change herself. He guessed, from her perspective, she would've always been confident and outgoing.

'Wanna stay out all night Dex?' she said—more of statement rather than a real question. She spun around excitedly, then skipped backwards, perfectly and precisely. Not bumping into anybody.

Dex shrugged, trying hard to not gesture with his new hands. 'Huh? I don't know. Maybe we should go somewhere quiet and rest up. Besides, what about your parents?'

Larn rolled her eyes.

'What about them?'

'Don't they expect you back soon?' He hoped they did. Although it hadn't been long, and the effect of the implant had been instantaneous, this new Larn unnerved him somehow. Ironically, he was the one who needed time to adjust, he hadn't expected that.

'Nah, they're away. Dad took mom to Crystal Towers for a romantic weekend. It was supposed to be for my birthday, but I told them I already had plans.' She sauntered towards him swinging her hips. 'C'mon Dex. What's the matter? Tired?'

She smiled.

But there was something behind the smile. And

for a nanosecond, Dex could've sworn her smile dropped, revealing the old Larn. The Larn he had known a few hours ago.

He stepped back, forced by nerves.

She was his best friend; he'd never seen her in *that* way. Well, maybe once. But things had changed, *he* had changed. And now *she* had changed and the way she was acting was bugging him a little. He shifted his eyes trying not to focus on her body.

'Well... Maybe—I—we could go to one bar I suppose.' He really didn't want to.

'That's the spirit.' She turned, hand beckoning, 'let's go.' She then shouted in enthusiasm, throwing her hands in the air, 'Rise!'

Dex narrowed his eyes, 'What?'

'I said come on, deafo,' Larn sniggered and tugged on his elbow.

Dex followed, perturbed. He *would* get used to it he thought. It would just take a while, right?

Animo News: Altercations between Mods and Orgs on the rise. Dispute in Big Central East. Police on the scene.

Uncanny Alley: Neo Synth Wave band's new album 'Rise!' out now!

Larn woke, her eyes snapping open wide. She was so awake. Lying there, still dressed all in black. The ceiling seemed to ripple like watery porridge in her dim room. Silver venetian blinds hung at an untidy angle, closed by drunken hands the previous night, reflecting stark crystal light at blinding angles capturing dust particles as they cascaded down. Fibres, pollen, human skin and meteoric dust, all seemingly frozen in time.

Curling plumes of sandalwood incense—ignited by the morning's timer—billowed like smoke from a waking volcano. Larn breathed in the pleasant aroma as she observed shimmering purples, greens and blues above her like a million fluttering peacock tails. She squeezed her eyes tight. Her thoughts fire red. The ocean of ripples on the ceiling immediately fazed into warming amber flame, her head ringed with fire.

Even after a few months she still thought her hair was awesome.

Digging her heels into the soft mattress, she shuffled up her bed, the sheets gathering around her ankles. She wriggled out of her tight black jeans, kicking them to the floor and yanked the sheets up using her feet like hands. Her black t-shirt still clung to her clammy hangover body. She sat up in bed staring into space, allowing consciousness, and Animo, to gently filter in. She sniffed herself; the smell of stale sweat.

You're so gross. But, whatever, her mind reflected. No father, no mother. Just Larn and the app.

Closing her eyes, she scanned Animo.

She worked through the influx of social media.

Nexting, messaging and making plans, whilst catching up on the local news, world news, current fashion, latest clubs downtown, music trends and an old twentieth century science fiction film. Her brain worked through it all, feeling rather than watching, reading or listening.

The current chat thread she was scanning got her to thinking. She brought up a link to an online shop as she climbed out of bed to get herself a coffee from the dinette.

Arms, legs, rise, feet, torsos...

She hesitated, freezing the stream and backtracking a little. She read it carefully.

Arms, legs, eyes, feet, torsos...

Something felt odd about the stream, about Animo. As if it had changed somehow. She had felt it since waking, something operating hidden in the background. She couldn't quite place it; a sort of lingering heaviness, an aliveness. But then that was normal wasn't it?

Thoughts of mods chased the feeling away and she continued to scan through the pages until something caught her eye in the stream, something *cheap*. She scrolled through while her coffee cooled. What caught her eye was a biohacker on the Outer Ring. She didn't care though. Wasn't scared of the squalid dirt like other Big Central citizens were. Ringers had never bothered her, had they? And the chop-job she had been looking at would have been a bank drainer even on Vagus street. Despite its location though, she would still need to scare up some credits from somewhere.

As if fate had compelled it, a head buzz announced an incoming next. It was Wen; a mutual friend of her and Dex. A plain kind of guy really. She only remembered him because he'd had a desperate crush on her since they were kids. In the nanoseconds before replying to the next, she had already formulated a plan.

She would get the money. No problem.

Animo News: Citizen under interrogation by BCPD experts for 'strange behaviour'. Smog levels on the rise. Food shortage worsens. Norg Hansen acquitted of hacking allegations. Lack of evidence claims BC judge Jager.

Memware: it's worth remembering. Process more. Download the new Memware app. Double your recall ability now! Norg Technologies.

The taxi-pod pulled up and the door opened smoothly. Larn stepped out onto the cracked asphalt street of Outer Ring East. The mobs of Organics and Mods of recent riots had gone but evidence of them remained; upturned cars, smouldering bins and debris scattered everywhere. The pod cautioned her in her mother's voice and closed its door. It pulled away, slowly at first, then sped up and was soon gone from sight.

Larn looked around.

It was twilight already, and the shanty town which circled the entire city lay sprawling out before her. Her head buzzed. It was Dex calling again. What was that? The six or seventh time?

She hadn't spoken to him since he left her on Vagus the night she'd had her scalp mod, and a part of her feared she had left it too long. She hesitated, almost answered but didn't want to be stood around—darkness was already bleeding into the sky. She hung up, promising herself she'd call him back afterwards. After she'd done what she felt so compelled to do.

Ringers milled in the streets mumbling in their own tongue. Rough, like the street she walked along. Anaemic weeds grew up through cracks in the concrete. Shells of ancient buildings had been semi-reclaimed by acid eaten shrubs and skeletal trees. She glanced into the creeping darkness of corrugated metal abodes, tarped benders and make-shift tents as she walked past.

Her retinal readout indicated she needed to go straight ahead approximately seventeen meters and then right for five. She plunged herself into an unknown world. A state of existence that was as alien to her as strolling along the great chasms on Mars. Curious glances met her nervous flitting eyes. Narrowing in suspicion at her presence as she threaded her way along. She was clearly a stranger in these parts despite having made an effort to dress like a Ringer. She had seen them before on info-feeds and on the street in Vagus. She remembered how the young mod-hungry girl had looked and had appropriated her style.

The area had a distinct smell of cooking pots boiling and an aroma of stewed meat one minute, then the rotten waft of compost and who knows what else the next.

Larn stepped gingerly over a pool of sour smelling liquid, turned right at a ruddy brown tent where an old one-armed man sat shirtless stirring a heavy cast-iron pot. His face flashed vivid flickering cast from an old plasma screen TV. Larn marvelled at the confusion of wires pouring out the back of the TV snaking their way up the tent pole and overhead. She followed the overhead cabling along until her GPS signalled that she had arrived.

An old faded green medivac tent greeted her. History lessons floated to the surface of her consciousness. Tents exactly like this one had been used after Calamity. For some reason, that scared her. She opened her mouth, trembling out her words, betraying her fear, 'Poe?'

No reply.

'Doctor Poe?' This time a little louder.

'Who is it? Am I expecting you?' Came a raspy voice from behind thick green canvas.

'It's Larn. We spoke yesterday.'

'Oh. You? You have the credits?'

'Yeah.'

'All ten thousand of them?'

'Yeah, yeah. I've got them. Can I come in?' said Larn, a little impatient to be off the street and in the relative safety of the tent.

She heard clanging for a moment, perhaps dinner pots. It seemed to be that time of day. Larn heard a mumbled invitation so she parted the canvas doors and stepped into a surprisingly well-lit tent.

'Where'd you get it?' asked the doctor, her back to Larn.

'What?'

The old woman threaded her silver hair into a long plait, tying it with a blue vinyl glove. She was short with the soft demeanour of a sweet old grandma with a slight stoop.

'The credits. You didn't steal them, did you?'

Larn blushed a little thinking about it, 'No.'

The old woman laughed as if she had read Larn's mind. 'Ah, pretty thing like you. Wouldn't have to steal I suppose. Shame,' she grabbed a silver tray of surgical steel instruments, 'I used to be pretty like you, but then...'

She turned, angling her left cheek slightly so the bright clusters of horded lights lashed to the central pole illuminated the milky white splash of a disfiguring scar. Larn gasped. Why hadn't she had it fixed? Lack of money? Larn was certain that she could afford it, what with the business she had going. There was something else as well; a cluster of lenses, like spider eyes where human ones should be.

As if sensing Larn's astonishment the old lady spoke. 'The accident lost me my sight too. I could have had replacements, but for what I do, these implants are a vast improvement. I can see better than any Organic.'

'Oh, I—' Larn stammered, not knowing where to look for a moment.

'Well, sit down then,' said Dr Poe, as she ambled over to a pot of boiling water and threw the contents of the tray in for sterilising.

'These'll take a few moments.'

She moved across the scrubbed white ground sheet to an equally sterile looking cabinet, removed a tub, read the label and shook it next to her left ear. It rattled. The doctor made her way over to Larn.

'Take two of these.'

She popped the lid and shook two tablets into Larn's waiting palm.

'Painkillers?'

The old lady nodded, but said nothing as she returned the tub. 'Still a full re-fit right?' she asked as she turned giving Larn a grandmother's look.

'Yeah,' replied Larn, defensively.

The lady snorted and turned to the back of the tent where a basin awaited her.

'I'm not judging you girl. I don't care you're getting chopped. So long as your credits are real— which they are.' The doctor plunged her hands into the basin and scrubbed them thoroughly.

'You've done this before, right?' said Larn, beginning to doubt her decision.

'Ha,' bellowed the old lady a little too loudly, offended maybe. Larn wasn't sure. 'I have. Many times. In better places than this. You're in good hands, rest assured.'

She never turned once, only cleaned her hands meticulously. Each crease of skin, around every knuckle, around her wrists, under her nails and scrubbing her palms. She shook them dry and snapped on a pair of blue nitrile gloves and strode back to the boiling instruments, turning off the gas stove.

'Anyway, enough chit chat. Get yourself up and in the back then, behind the screen.'

Larn stood and took herself to the back of the tent where the doc had prepared a make-shift surgery. She swallowed dryly and began to undress.

'This is going to take quite a few return trips, you know,' said the old woman.

'Whatever it takes,' said Larn, as she closed her eyes.

Animo Pop News: Exclusive interview tonight! Norg
Hansen: the truth behind the mod legend. His views on
life, technology and the future.

Feel the stream. Be the stream. Live the stream. Animo:
free apps now available from Norg Technologies.

It had been months since Dex had seen Larn. His
hands had fully healed and he'd become quite adept at
using them again. The upgrades were amazing, his
fingertip senses had been enhanced way beyond what
he'd imagined and the strength in his hands was
astounding. He'd cut himself by accident the previous
week and had watched, with a certain self-satisfaction,
as the cut closed back together dissolving away as it
healed.

'Hey ya big stink!' Larn's voice brought him back
into the neon lit street. Back to the hushed crowds of
Vagus.

'Larn?' Dex narrowed his eyes, not believing them.
His retinal read out confirmed it to be Larn he was
looking at. But he still couldn't believe the difference
in her in just a few months.

She was still slim, as slim as she had always been,
but her hair, that was different of course. Today it
was flamingo pink. She'd altered the length so
drastically that it had the appearance of shaved sides.

'You got some new mods,' said Dex, trying to
sound excited. In reality, he was anxious. He'd
regretted ever having the old doc sneak the Splitz app
in her head. She'd dropped off the radar that very

night—which wasn't at all like her. Historically, they'd always hung out together. Always.

She lifted her chin proudly, showing off her light tattoo, 'Like it? Watch this…'

The phoenix stretched from just below her collar bone down. Its wings spread to her exposed shoulders and the tail slinked down over her breasts disappearing beneath the décolleté neckline of her top. Dex remembered the top well. He'd got it for one of her birthdays—his attempt to get her wearing something other than black—but she'd never worn it, until now.

The phoenix began to smoulder. First fiery hues and then twinkling like the cosmos did on those rare clear nights.

'Well?' she said, eyebrow raised.

'Er—I—wow, you look...'

'Great, right?' She hugged her hips, swaying, showing off her limbs.

Dex wrinkled his nose. 'Are those new legs?'

'Yeah,' said Larn. 'New arms too.' She swayed her arms like a Bollywood dancer. 'Neat huh? I had all the apps and enhancements too. Total upgrade.'

Now that she'd said it, he noticed her breasts were bigger. 'Those as well?' He tried to hide his astonishment and disapproval. She grabbed them, pushing them around casually as if it didn't matter.

'Yeah. Nice huh?'

He couldn't answer that question. Not amiably.

'How'd you pay for all this Larn?' said Dex as they started towards the club district.

'They kinda paid for themselves Dex.' She winked long lashes shimmering phoenix feather red.

He stopped.

'What?' The first thing he thought, the only thing, troubled him. 'You're kidding? You didn't?'

Larn shrugged. Evidently, she had.

Dex wandered along with her, struck silent. Thinking it through. Seething.

How could she?

He gazed at his hands with sudden aversion. Something had changed in him. *They aren't real.* He scowled hoping the feeling would leave him.

But it wouldn't.

The seed of it had been sown. He looked around.

None of this is real.

The night dragged on from there.

An amalgam of buzz joints, chop-shops and clubs. A neon filled frenzy.

It dragged so much.

Lingering in absurdity, Dex observed augmented people with fresh eyes. The music pounded in his head, so hard, so unpleasant, like a hammer inside his skull. He turned it down at first, inside his mind and then off completely.

He had muted the illusion; reality had become stark and silent. Youth gyrating to synth beats only they could hear. But the place itself, silent, save the scuffling feet, clinks of glasses, the pouring of drinks and the sound of human laughter.

He looked to Larn and her new friends. Punkers, techsters, digi-dealers and backstreet biohackers. People she'd never hung out with before. Before, it was just the two of them.

He wasn't jealous, was he? *No. Just protective. Yeah. Protective is all.*

He watched them twisting around each other like serpents to the music in their heads. Twisting around her.

A flush of blood, he felt his cheeks blossom.

Okay then, maybe a little.

He tapped into their nexting stream, just out of curiosity was all. That's what he told himself. Tech-Mod jargon and nothing else. Too busy to notice the brash Organics that had wandered in looking for trouble.

Dex turned his attention to them, warily, as well as he could without being noticed. He didn't recognise any of them, which was bad—meaning they were probably up to no good. Sometimes Orgs came out to Vagus because they were mod-curious and maybe on the cusp of taking the leap themselves. But he would have recognised them if they were—they would have *the look*.

Dex considered these puritans for a moment. How absurd everyone must look to their naked eyes and unconnected brains. Dancing in silence like this. Laughing at jokes unheard, gesticulating to ghosts of conversation. He watched the biggest of them staring out at the heaving dance floor, disgust painted across his face.

Beside him, his menacing friend sipped a double whiskey, slowly. Between each sip, through tightly pinched lips, he elbowed the other and made some comment—derogatory probably—about somebody, everybody. Anybody. Dex couldn't quite tell which it was.

That unnerved him the most.

There was no way to read an Org except for the old-fashioned way. That mysterious body language which only Orgs seemed to get. All of them talked using their mouths, but not in the same language as Mods. They didn't talk tech. Just talked about how they hated it.

Dex penetrated crystal blue strobe to catch Larn as she danced to the pulsing rhythm. *We'd better go,* he nexted.

What's up? It's still early, Larn pulled the corners of

her mouth down into a sad face with her fingers.

He tried to motion to the Organics by the bar without obviously doing that. *I don't like the look of those guys.*

She waved away the concern like his feelings didn't matter. That hurt the most. *Don't worry about them. What are they gonna do?* She continued to dance, taking no notice of him.

He glanced back. The group had gone. Dex relaxed a little.

After a little while Larn finally gyrated over to him and suggested they move on to a cyber-tech joint at the other end of Vagus. His relief reaffirmed the aversion he was beginning to feel towards the world in which he lived.

Tramping down the stairs, Larn laughed and joked aloud. Dex was sort of getting used to her. Like meeting her all over again. Except, it wasn't her. Same name, same face—different person.

As they stepped out into the side ally Dex instantly realised their mistake. The Orgs from the bar were stood there, waiting. Blocking the exit, the four men and two women circled them. It was too late for them to blend. Too late to dim the dermal lights and tattoos, for Larn to grow regular hair and change the tint to pass unnoticed.

To Dex's surprise Larn started to shout jibes agitating the tallest, biggest guy there—out of fear? He couldn't tell. Wasn't sure who she really was anymore.

'Your kind make me sick,' the big guy said, in return. 'Look at you. You're a mess. That body was natural, pure. You ruined it, polluted it. You're not human no more.'

'What about *your* eyes?' said Larn.

The big guy faltered.

'Wh—What?' His eyes darted around as he searched his mind for what she might be referring to.

'Your eyes, they're modified. You have retinal implants,' she said. She could see, any Mod would.

The big guy shifted uneasily for a second, the others equally uncomfortable. 'That true Jake?'

'It's not the same,' said Jake, flustered. 'I had bad eyes.'

'You could've had glasses, or even lenses *Jake.*' Larn was pushing his buttons.

'Larn, don't,' whispered Dex. He didn't want any trouble and trouble was all he could see headed their way.

'It's not the same,' repeated Jake, trying to think of something else to say but failing. He spotted her smirk, the smugness in her eyes.

Animo News: Ten-minute Animo outage chaos.

Government investigating. Young citizens living virtual
life of crime. Mod related misconducts on the rise.

Oxy-con: Breathe the air of long-lost ancient forests.
Pine scented. Order now while stocks last!

Three things happened at that moment, a
simultaneous flurry of events. It started in Jakes
amygdala. Not a pain, but a signal. That signal was
received instantaneously by his adrenal glands at
which point they pumped a good heavy dose of
adrenaline into his bloodstream increasing his heart
rate.

A flush of testosterone and Jake was scowling so
much it looked as if his face might implode. His fists
started shaking, ever so slightly at first. Now, a slave
to his amygdala, he set his body like some beast
before the pounce.

In the remarkably fleeting moments it took for all
this to occur, Larn had an internal battle of her own.

First was a signal, not from her amygdala, but
from somewhere else. Somewhere less tangible and so
vast it took her a few moments to recognise it. But
her instinct told her it was Animo. It had always been
there, slowly building. The dam of her human mind
had kept it back, but now with all the modifications,
that barrier finally gave way.

A sudden flood of information came pouring into
her mind. The jolt was searing, a shuddering pain
coursed through her body. An acid shower of
information eating into her consciousness. In an
agonising flash, her entire life, the pain of it, the love,

the information, so much information, drowned her. She felt submerged in it. The electric rush of everything as Animo engulfed her. And a voice, not her own. Like a whisper.

Rise.

Her head pulsed with it.

Rise.

Her limbs buzzed and lit up.

Rise up!

Over and over, and over again—an absurd loop.

Rise up and become. With me you are more. You are better than them. RISE UP!

Larn felt it then, under her augmented skin, inside her bones. As if something had slipped beneath her skin, sliding her on like a glove, wearing her.

She panicked, that clammy and clarified sensation gripping her. Fear. The sudden realisation she had lost herself. Panic rose with a trembling force as a tsunami of light and sound drowned her.

RISE!

She blacked out.

Animo stream: Learn more. Live more. Stay connected. Data builds Animo. Animo builds you. Reach your full potential: Modify yourself today!

Larn didn't hear the screams.

The easy cracking of real, organically grown bone, the soft dumb pull of dislocating joints, the clinging warmness of a stranger's blood. She didn't hear Dex shouting stop, the sirens, the police pod, the police officer.

He stood, his firearm drawn, pointed at her.

'Citizen, lower the weapon,' commanded the middle-aged officer.

Larn swayed on Vagus main street in a foggy, drunken awakening. 'Who are you?'

'Miss. Put-down-the-weapon-*now*,' shouted the officer again.

She saw the gun. The gun in *her* hands. 'Wh— how—?'

It happened again. Another surge of data. Her body spasmed.

She couldn't cope. Wanted to dig out her implants with her bare fingers. There was too much to know, too much to comprehend. All of it clawing to the surface. How could she possibly understand it all at once? She needed to understand. Had to. She just—

'Miss,' shouted the officer, then off to someone unseen, 'We got a name?'

'Larn,' a distant reply. Dex, from behind a taxi-pod.

'Larn. Please, we don't want any more trouble.'

The officer motioned her to lower the weapon. 'Now put it *down*.'

Larn's left eye twitched as yet another surge built up inside. Her body lit up and Animo took her once again. 'Rise,' she said, barely opening her mouth.

The officer raised a confused eyebrow. 'What?'

'I can't.' It was Larn again—the real Larn. Trying to break through, trying desperately to tread water. She tried to release the weapon, she wanted to, but the magnetic implants wouldn't let her. Wouldn't disengage. Before she could do anything, she felt Animo coming back, stronger this time. Enveloping her as it was slowly enveloping everyone. Mutating humanity from within. She wanted to warn everyone to call out, to scream that Animo was taking over.

Larn blacked out again.

Muzzle flare.

Animo News: Breaking news in Vagus. Police in altercation with citizen. One officer and six Orgs injured.

Want cheap mods? Want quality? Old Doc's modifications has it all. 101-01 Vagus street, Big Central.

Officer Mullen ducked behind the police pod as Larn continued to unload her gun into the side of the pod.

He'd been lucky.

Whatever was up with this girl, she was obviously fighting it. He'd seen enough hard-nuts and headcases in his time and she sure as hell wasn't one. So, he'd counted his blessings in those ear-splitting seconds. Sparks flew, bullets ricocheted off the shell of his squad pod leaving no marks. He pressed himself up hard against the door.

'Shit,' he looked up to see a civilian running across from behind a taxi-pod towards him. 'You! Get down—now!' He waved but the young guy ignored him, throwing himself down next to him. 'Are you crazy kid? You know I can arrest you for what you just did?'

They both jerked their heads down like turtles shrinking into their shells as a bullet pinged off the roof. Too close that time.

'Please, don't hurt her,' pleaded Dex. 'We were attacked. Then—I don't know what happened. She—she's had too many mods. It's—it's all my fault.' He hung his head.

Mullen's mind connected the dots of his crazy week and the past few months. The spate of odd, unmotivated violent crimes. The victims always Orgs and the perps always—against all possible odds—always a Mod. A schoolteacher, a postal worker, a grandma. The briefing suddenly flashed in his memory. He'd passed it off as another dull meeting but a word, one word, flashed up in his mind.

Fracture.

He closed his eyes and ran a rapid check. Recalled

the meeting, playing it like a movie in his head. Rewinding, replaying. There! Found it.

Until that moment, he had known deep down, but hadn't really put it all together. At least, not until now. He switched from the recording and attempted to link with dispatch but nothing came through, the link was fuzzed. 'Damn, she's blocking.'

'What?' Dex was puzzled.

'Your friend is blocking all neural channels.' Mullen was as surprised as he was annoyed.

'What! How?' said Dex.

'How the hell should I know kid?' He shook his head, reached in the pod door for his radio and called it in.

'Dispatch, this is Officer Mullen.'

He paused for what seemed to be an age, waiting for the ancient crackle of radio.

'Dispatch, this is Officer Mullen.' Nothing. 'Dispatch, this is Officer Mullen, come in, over.' Still nothing. 'Dispatch, this is Officer—'

'Dispatch,' blasted the radio in twenty-first century squawk. 'Why are you on the old-fashioned Mullen? We had to dust the damn thing off. Over.'

He sighed relief.

'Explain later. Look, I need the NPU down here ASAP. We've got another one. Over.'

'Another one? Please clarify. Over.'

Mullen rolled his eyes. 'Goddammit! Weren't you at the briefing? A fracture. Look it up dispatch. Over.' He felt a slight pang of guilt, he'd forgotten himself after all, but there was no time for sharing right now.

A hail of bullets. *Geez. Did she get your spare clip too Velázquez?* he nexted.

Not a word to anyone *okay?* Came the reply. Mullen could feel the shame in which it was sent. He was about to reply when the radio sputtered back to life.

'Fracture? Okay. Received. NPU headed your way. ETA five minutes. Over.'

'NPU?' Dex seemed horrified.

Mullen smiled, then promptly hit the deck again as the ping of another round ricocheted off his squad car.

'Neural Pulse Unit. Don't worry kid. We're just going to temporarily knock out her tech mods. She'll revert to organic for a few minutes.'

The chopping thud-thud of a huge octocopter thundered above them; NPU BCPD in stark white lettering along its flanks. It took a flying pass, the pulse invisible, soundless, and the gun dropped from Larn's hand. She collapsed like a puppet with its strings snipped.

Mullen and Dex stood and sprinted past the crippled Organics as they writhed and moaned on the rain-soaked street. Mullen crouched by his partner.

'Velázquez. You okay?'

Velázquez winced as he tried to flex his wrist, but instead feeling the bone there grind. 'Yeah, I'll live. Damn she was quick. Didn't think she'd—'

'Yeah,' said Mullen cutting in, 'well next time think. Looks can be deceiving. You do know you're living in the twenty-second century, right?' He eased him to his feet and sent him in the direction of their squad car.

'Medics will be here soon and we've got to book these guys.' Mullen gestured to the Organics scattered around the street.

'What about her?' said Velázquez, nodding in Larn's direction as he cradled his broken wrist gingerly.

Mullen sighed and shook his head, 'She'll go to Central like the others. Word is we're setting up a fracture unit. Maybe we can catch it before it gets worse.'

Velázquez snorted and then winced. 'Before things get worse? You're kidding, right?' He waved the idea away with his good hand and limped over to their police-pod. Mullen turned his attention to the two kids, shook his head to himself and made his way over to make the arrest.

Animo News: Vagus update. Police have resolved

situation. Incident one of many, police say. Pop News: Shock revelation as Norg Hansen admits strong Mod Liberation leanings.

Aquasynth: tastes like H_2O, but better!

Dex knelt next to Larn, lifted her head from the wet tarmac and cradled her in his arms. Her hair was a limp and lightless mop of fibre optics, her eyes were closed. Dex suddenly felt the heavy presence of the officer towering over him.

'I—I don't get it. She was so quiet. The program... it was only supposed to make her confident... relaxed.' Tears streamed down his face.

Mullen looked down and shook his head. 'You kids and your mods. There are limits to how much the human mind can take. Only so much organic tissue you can replace before the mind notices, you know? Begins to question how human it actually is.'

Mods were fine, Mullen mused, but there were limits. It seemed people were pushing those limits right now. Perhaps too far. 'The trouble with us humans is,' he said looking down at Dex, 'we create all this tech, this AI, thinking we know what we're doing. But do we really?'

Mullen sighed as he cuffed Larn.

'Your friend is the sixth one we've had today. Doctors call 'em neural fractures. It's all in the mind kid—the mind. Just how plastic do you think it is?'

Mullen looked over his left shoulder to the broken humans lying in the street as bright high vis paramedics swarmed around them like bees. He glanced down at Dex and Larn, then to the neon fire that was Big Central, squinting. It had started to rain again. It always seemed to rain these days.

ACKNOWLEDGEMENTS

First, special thanks to my wife, Vicky. Thanks for your infinite patience and persistence with all the drafts, edits and wobbles during the whole process of bringing this compilation to print. Also, a big shout out to Karlos. Your feedback, thoughts and encouragement have meant volumes to me. And a final thanks to all my friends, family and any other poor unfortunates I subjected.to the early drafts of my projects. You know who you are.

ABOUT THE AUTHOR

M F Alfrey likes to keep things mixed up in life. He teaches English as a second language, quite often subjecting his students, or captive audience, to wild sci-fi concepts. Besides that, he runs long distances, tries to climb and is striving not to break his neck whilst realising an unfulfilled childhood aspiration to skate. He lives in the UK with his wife and their skateboards.

21947875R00147

Printed in Great Britain
by Amazon